Donald MacKenzie and The Murder Room

>>> This title is part of The Murder Room, our series dedicated to making available out-of-print or hard-to-find titles by classic crime writers.

Crime fiction has always held up a mirror to society. The Victorians were fascinated by sensational murder and the emerging science of detection; now we are obsessed with the forensic detail of violent death. And no other genre has so captivated and enthralled readers.

Vast troves of classic crime writing have for a long time been unavailable to all but the most dedicated frequenters of second-hand bookshops. The advent of digital publishing means that we are now able to bring you the backlists of a huge range of titles by classic and contemporary crime writers, some of which have been out of print for decades.

From the genteel amateur private eyes of the Golden Age and the femmes fatales of pulp fiction, to the morally ambiguous hard-boiled detectives of mid twentieth-century America and their descendants who walk our twenty-first century streets, The Murder Room has it all. **>>>**

The Murder Room
Where Criminal Minds Meet

themurderroom.com

Donald MacKenzie 1908–1994

Donald MacKenzie was born in Ontario, Canada, and educated in England, Canada and Switzerland. For twenty-five years MacKenzie lived by crime in many countries. 'I went to jail,' he wrote, 'if not with depressing regularity, too often for my liking.' His last sentences were five years in the United States and three years in England, running consecutively. He began writing and selling stories when in American jail. 'I try to do exactly as I like as often as possible and I don't think I'm either psychopathic, a wayward boy, a problem of our time, a charming rogue. Or ever was.'

He had a wife, Estrela, and a daughter, and they divided their time between England, Portugal, Spain and Austria.

Raven in Flight

Donald MacKenzie

An Orion book

Copyright © The Estate of Donald MacKenzie 1976

The right of Donald MacKenzie to be identified as the author of this work has
been asserted in accordance with the Copyright, Designs and Patents Act 1988.

This edition published by
The Orion Publishing Group Ltd
Orion House
5 Upper St Martin's Lane
London WC2H 9EA

An Hachette UK company
A CIP catalogue record for this book is available from the British Library

ISBN 978 1 4719 0499 8

www.orionbooks.co.uk

A book for Joanna, who gives me understanding, desire and a hand in the night.

I STRETCHED my legs, pushing the driving seat back as far as it would go. It's difficult to find a car to fit me since I'm made on the order of a dragonfly, six feet four inches tall and narrow shouldered. Anyway it was June and the hot Atlantic sun had burnished my face and bleached out my hair. It's normally gray white and Sweeny Todd styles it so that it falls over the ears and collar. People either like the production or they don't. It's been a long time since I really cared, one way or the other. Lilac-colored trousers and a T-shirt covered the jellyfish stings on my legs and stomach but I knew they were there.

My sandals were on the back seat. I poked with a bare foot, trying out the clutch and brake pedals. It was obvious that the mechanic washing his hands across the yard had made no attempt to clean the car. It was Saturday afternoon and late. The floorboards were scratchy with sand, the ashtray crammed with lipsticked cigarette butts. I leaned out of the windows and emptied them pointedly onto the ground. The mechanic grinned, gave me the two fingers and mounted his scooter. He left the yard in a cloud of dust. It was hot in spite of the hour. I checked the gauges on the dashboard. The small white Seat was the same model as the one I'd been hiring for the last six weeks.

There was no one left in the yard but the girl standing in the office doorway. She was an improbable redhead and spoke English and tied her blouse instead of buttoning it.

I stared hard at her flat brown belly. "Do you think I can rely on this thing? I've been fooling around with that slipping clutch for the last couple of weeks, you know."

She made the nasal hum of the Spaniard just about to launch into English. "I am sure, Señor. A lady just return it!"

I wasn't too sure what that meant but I shifted my gaze to her eyes. The world-weary older-man pose had been known to pay dividends with her generation. Her polite smile dismissed my unspoken invitation. I noticed for the first time that her legs were crooked and she was chewing gum. I gave her back her smile.

"Well, thanks anyway for staying behind, and enjoy your weekend!"

I took a right turn onto the one straight street in the sprawling village. Las Ventas was basically still a fishing settlement with squat whitewashed houses set around the hoop of bay-like nail holes in a horseshoe. Men were sleeping along the *embarcadero* in the shade of upturned boats. When the season finished in October, the youths who had worked as waiters would be back mending the fishnets. The old would huddle in doorways and patios, serene in the winter sunshine, the strangeness of the summer forgotten.

A red traffic signal guarded the entrance to the Plaza Mayor. A cop in a soiled white tunic, rope-soled shoes and a sun helmet operated the controls from the safety of the sidewalk. Orange trees enclosed the square, the sharp fragrance of the still-green fruit mingling with the smells of seaweed and diesel fuel. I propped my elbows on the steering wheel and lit a Ducados. The tiled square was empty except for a drunk sleeping it off on a beach and some small girls playing mysteriously. The red and yellow Spanish flag hung in folds over the marble-fronted bank. The water in the fountain jetted fitfully through the mouths of stone dolphins. I reflected that this probably meant another cold bath. When the water pressure was low the gas heaters in the bungalows didn't work. Six weeks in Las Ventas had taught me that nothing could be taken for granted. Like the episode with the French girl the week before. We'd met in the bar, Wolfie Field making the introductions.

"This is ex-Detective-Inspector Raven, Monique." He'd given me a large grin to go with the wink. "Monique's a writer with a passion for cops."

She was a slightly bucktoothed journalist with Parisian chic and a well-developed bust. After a surfeit of the mauve-and blue-rinsed matrons who spaced their consumption of gin with complaints about the waiters' breath she came as a godsend. I'd spun the evening out, banging on about life at the Yard and lying my head off. By the time I took her back to the bungalow for a nightcap I was already wondering how I could get rid of her before morning. Three minutes later some clown in the local powerhouse kicked a switch and all the lights went out. We sat there, uneasily silent in a darkness that had come too soon for both of us. Finally I walked her back to the club. As we reached the entrance the lights came on again, just in time for me to read the amusement in her eyes. It revised my thinking entirely and I spent the rest of the night sucking indigestion pills. She left for Cádiz the following day. As Field pointed out, there is no such thing as justice, especially for ex-cops.

The policeman on the pavement flicked his cigarette end into the gutter and signaled the change from red to green with a piercing blast on his whistle. There was no one but me waiting. Three dogs barked and the drunk on the bench shifted position. I pressed a calloused sole on the accelerator. It was a good way to drive and after weeks of going barefoot I no longer charged across the burning sand in agony. I'd taken to selecting isolated beaches where there was no one to observe me floating in naked boredom. So there I'd be, surrounded by shoals of coelenterates, reflecting that I was almost forty years of age, no ties and enough money of my own to tell the Commissioner of Police to go fuck himself and all it added up to was boredom.

"Has the nose and instincts of a weasel," someone had scribbled on one of my reports from police college all those years ago. It was just another way of saying that the only thing that ever really turned me on was and is the chase. The chase of the human being. It's a firmly lodged foible that got me onto the Force and then off it.

I leaned hard on the horn, glowering, as an indifferent urchin in minute swimtrunks sauntered in front of the car. These days the little bastards don't even want to grow up and shoulder their share of trouble. The small Seat climbed out of the village, up the side of a hill thick with umbrella pines. The banks of the hardtop road were lined with cactus, dusty gray green plants with inch-long thorns. Country club lore had it that a guest had been thrown on the like from his horse and subsequently divorced by a dissatisfied wife.

A horn sounded behind. A green Peugeot station wagon showed in the rearview mirror, close on my tail. The driver was signaling me to pull over. I braked, switched off the ignition and started a cigarette. The tall man coming from the Peugeot was shirtless and wearing tennis shorts and sneakers. He pushed his blond curly head through the open window and grinned engagingly. A gold articulated fish swung on a chain around his neck.

"Hi!"

"Hi!" I said guardedly. His wrestler's shoulders were deeply suntanned and he was wearing blue eye shadow.

"Don't shoot!" he said, holding up a hand. "I'm Jerry Abbott. It's Mr. Raven, isn't it?" His voice was pleasant, the American accent negligible.

"Right," I admitted. It was a strange place for a pickup but these days who could tell.

Abbott's smile spread, crinkling the skin around his eyes. "The Garage Central. I just missed you. I chased the girl up

4

and she gave me your name."

I nodded. "I'm driving the wrong car."

He shook his head. If his curls had been longer they'd have sprayed all over the place.

"No. It's just that a friend of mine has been using this car over the last few days while I was in Madrid. As a matter of fact she only turned it in a couple of hours ago. And naturally she left her purse."

He pointed at the corner of the dash. I reached across and lifted the soft fold of red leather. I weighed it in my palm for a second, feeling the angled hardness of the keys inside. Abbott picked the purse from my outstretched hand and wriggled an eyebrow.

"That's women for you!"

I shrugged, feeling along the top of the dashboard. There was a pack of cigarettes, Sullivan Powell Virginia Rounds, a reminder of *Raffles*. E. W. Hornung's book about the cricket-playing society cracksman had been fascinating reading for a sixth former intent on joining the constabulary. I gave the cigarettes to Abbott and looked back over my shoulder. There was nothing on the rear seat except my sandals.

"That seems to be it," I said.

He pulled back, the gold fish swinging on his broad chest. "Thanks a lot, Mr. Raven. You know the way it is, a gal without her bits and pieces. The weekend would have been unendurable."

He held his smile for a couple of seconds and then turned away. I let the clutch in, looked up in the mirror as I went into the bend. He was leaning against the Peugeot, staring after me. At that distance and forgetting the eye shadow there was a suggestion of Steve McQueen about him.

An archway gapped the whitewashed walls that marked the boundaries of Las Ventas Country Club. The sixteen bungalows were placed discreetly among the umbrella pines. The club buildings, bar and restaurant, and Wolfie Field's private apartment were up on the crest of the hill. I swung the

Seat onto the sandy lane that led down to my bungalow. It had a red tiled roof and white walls veiled in bougainvillea. The pine trees grew close to a patch of brilliant Bermuda grass. Red ants made the grass impossible to lie on. The beach was a quarter-mile away, through a door in the wall and across the coastal highway. The club itself was no more than half that distance. I drove the Seat under the bamboo shelter and lit another cigarette. The only sound to disturb the peace was the metallic scrape of a male cicada's wings.

2

THE CURTAINS were drawn, which meant that the maids had been and gone. Apparently custom obliged them to work in pairs. The bungalow was one of the smaller ones and simple in design, no more than a couple of rooms and a bath. Thick walls kept the interior cool even in the heat of the day. There was a refrigerated drinks-dispenser but no kitchen. The maids brought breakfast from the club. It was the only meal served in the bungalows.

I searched my pockets uselessly for my sunglasses, then thumbed open the glove compartment. My hand was already inside before I remembered that I had turned one car in and taken another. My fingers closed on two booklets. I found myself looking at gold lettering on a green cover: UNITED STATES OF AMERICA. The passport was issued in the name of Gail Degenhardt, born in Hollister, California on April 13, 1946. The photograph attached showed an attractive-looking woman with dark shoulder-length hair smiling directly into the camera. It was a sensual face with confident eyes. I flipped the pages curiously. The immigration stamps on it showed that the holder had been in Czechoslovakia, Germany and England. There was an entry at Stansted Airport, an exit from the same place. The last franking was Spanish. *Aeropuerto de San Sebastián. Dirección General de Seguridad. Estrangeros.* The date was May 3, 1975.

I opened the international driver's license. The same face smiled at me from the inside of the back cover. Only this time the name was different. Giselle Dale, born in Hollister, April 3, 1946. I stuffed both documents back in the glove compartment. Whatever else, Miss Degenhardt-Dale was consistent in her choice of initials.

I unfastened the door and sat on the edge of the car, dangling my bare feet in the soft dirt. "Apply logic," as my Coordinator at Scotland Yard used to say. She was either Gail Degenhardt or Giselle Dale, hardly both. Not that I cared too much. I'd had enough trouble over the last year or so without going looking for it. I suppose it was the outrageousness of the situation that intrigued me. A woman of some apparent style and means using an alias, accompanied by the All-American wearing blue eye shadow.

Wasps were crawling in the dribble of water oozing from the end of the hosepipe. I watched them blankly, thinking of the woman's face. I didn't have to look at the photograph again to remember. The half-closed eyes and full-lipped mouth were already part of my memory. After a while I went inside.

The bungalow was simply furnished with cane chairs and tables, chintz curtains and cushions and grass mats spread on the red brick floors. The rough plastered walls were bright with sporting prints, the two fireplaces showing signs of winter use. I walked through to the bedroom and pulled back the curtains. The Hardy fishing rod I had brought was still in its case on top of a cupboard. I'd used it just once, snapping my line on the rocks and damn near breaking my back retrieving it. My sister had warned me that I'd be a lousy fisherman. *Stick to what you know,* she'd warned. *Ride a bicycle or something but don't make*

*a fool of yourself trying to catch fish. You don't have the
right sort of temperament.*

The bed had been turned down for the night, my
pajamas draped across a folded triangle of sheet. They
were white silk with a red lion embroided on the breast
pocket. A woman I once shared my bed with suggested
that the embroidery was flash. But I'd bought the pajamas
myself and the lion happens to be my birth sign. It seemed
to me that people who managed to get that close to me
should reserve their opinions.

The only communication I had with the two fat maids
was by way of nods and smiles and the occasional one-
hundred peseta note. There was a fair amount of nocturnal
traffic in and around the club. Cheap champagne is a great
solvent. There were parties of midnight bathers, married
women hanging out of convertibles trying to look like
strippers, a lot of splashing and shrieking. I was down on
the beach one night and watched an E-type Jaguar driven
down to the edge of the water and left there. A child could
have seen that the tide was coming in, not going out.
There were four of them, a couple of advertising agency
executives and their girl friends, doing some sort of leaping and prancing number a few hundred yards away. By
the time they came back, their car was hub deep in the
ocean. Nor would it start. It took twelve hours and the
club tractor to get the Jaguar out. A lot of it was my mood
but all this alcoholic exuberance left me completely indifferent. There seemed to be no percentage in exchanging
one form of boredom for another.

Very little happened at Las Ventas Country Club that
escaped the staff. For instance I knew that the maids worried about my solitary life-style. They'd shown an obvious
interest in the picture of my sister and her two children,
polishing the silver frame with their aprons and clucking.
Plainly they saw me as the victim of some deep domestic
disaster. I fished a couple of bottles of beer out of the
refrigerated dispenser. The Spaniards produced a lager that

9

is strong and full of flavor like their cigarettes. I'd been hooked on both ever since my arrival. I took the bottles out onto the terrace and slumped into a cane-bottomed chair. My throat worked thirstily as the chilly bubbles exploded. Suddenly dust lifted through the pine trees. I heard the rush of tires, a car door slam in front of the bungalow. It was Abbott's voice.

"Mr. Raven?"

I put my glass down. "Back here. On the terrace."

He came around the side of the house, shading his eyes. He was still shirtless, his wide tanned shoulders swinging as he crossed the grass. He put his hands on his hips and grinned down at me.

"This is getting to be a habit."

I pushed a chair in his direction with my foot. His reappearance came as no surprise. The woman would have remembered the passport and driver's license.

"You look as though you could use a beer," I suggested.

He made no move to sit down. "Thanks just the same. Guess what!"

I shrugged self-consciously. I'm thin and I'm aware of it. "I've no idea."

"We missed her passport," he said brightly.

I had the impression that I was supposed to fall about laughing. "Passport," I repeated. "You're quite sure you won't?" I offered the full bottle again.

"Absolutely." Abbott's casual glance skimmed the terrace and jumped through the open window into my bedroom. "She left her God damn passport in the glove compartment along with her driver's license. You didn't see them?"

I shook my head. "But then I didn't look for them."

"Of course not," he said quickly. "Come to that they could be anywhere. But we've looked in the house and she swears she remembers leaving them in the glove compartment. You don't mind if I check?" He hesitated momentarily as if he'd been wrong-footed in some way or another. "I really do apologize for disturbing you again."

I nodded across at the bamboo shelter. "Help yourself. The car's unlocked."

I watched curiously as he hurried away like a small boy released from school. He was definitely nervous. It showed in his eyes, his eagerness to be anywhere other than standing there talking to me. Whichever way you looked at it, though, a passport was an important document, kosher or not.

He trotted out of the carport, holding up the green booklet for me to see. "Found it!" he yelled triumphantly. "And her driver's license as well!"

I nodded congratulation. "That's good. Then you're off the hook."

An expression of malice replaced the debonair smile. "It isn't *me*, I'm not in the habit of making a God damn fool of myself."

"I don't know," I said comfortably. It was like being back in the charge room listening to some villain lying his head off with the evidence you need to convict him safely in your right-hand pocket. "It's the sort of thing that can happen to any of us."

He had a trick of shutting his eyes briefly as if thinking, then smiling as he opened them again. In a woman it would have been coquettish. The combination of blue eye shadow and muscled torso made the ploy somewhat sinister.

"You're not likely to be in the bar later this evening?" he asked. "I'd like to introduce you to the gal who's responsible for all this upheaval. We're dining in the restaurant."

I scratched my jellyfish stings tenderly. They itched like hell in spite of the drenching with calomel lotion. His invitation was casually made but I had a strong feeling that he wanted it accepted. I gave him the frank open look of a man you'd be glad to introduce to your girl friend.

11

"I'm usually in the bar any time after eight," I said. "To tell the honest truth I haven't found much else to do in the evenings."

"Great!" he said heartily. "Then we'll look forward to seeing you later." He raised a hand in farewell. Seconds later the dust rose through the trees again.

I sat on the terrace, eyes half-closed in the sunshine, listening to the dwindling sound of the motor. It was half-past seven when I went inside. I showered in tepid water and put on a pair of lightweight velvet trousers and a striped shirt from Mr. Fish. I'd bought the white shoes in Rome a couple of years before. A man living alone gets used to the face in the mirror. It's the only check he has on his appearance. I decided that I was gray and gaunt but interesting. I pulled the shades and closed the windows to keep out the mosquitoes and locked the front door behind me. The patches of Bermuda grass were emerald green after their evening soaking. I reminded myself to tell Field that we could do with less water on the grass and more in the bungalows.

Las Ventas County Club sprawled over 500 acres. Most of it was sand and the ubiquitous umbrella pines. As a one-time gambler on sporting events, Wolfie Field was proud of his six hard courts, 100-foot swimming pool and the putting green. He was even proud of the iron-mouthed Arabs in his riding stable. The club buildings clustered around an inner patio where drinks were served from the bar. The architect had spent some time in Mexico and, as Wolfie admitted, the place looked like a Warner Brothers set circa 1940. There were brightly colored woven rugs, chunky crucifixes set in wall embrasures, bar stools fashioned like western saddles. The restaurant windows faced the sunset and a backdrop of gum trees, a boon to romantically minded couples. Wolfie's private apartment overlooked the putting green. The maids and waiters lived in the village. The one exception was Domingo, the barman. He was an ex-bullfighter with perforated eardrums who'd taught himself to lip-read in Spanish and English.

Wolfie Field's admiration of Hemingway and Ruark showed in the way he'd decorated the public rooms. Stuffed birds of prey and animals done to death in the Sierra Nevada loomed from the walls of the entrance hall. The bar was a long bright room hung with nineteenth-century bullfight posters, and the saddle stools and couches were upholstered in scarlet leather. The shelves under the enormous baroque mirror were stacked with the most comprehensive selection of alcoholic beverages south of Madrid. I counted no less than seven brands of imported vodka and eighteen varieties of malt whisky.

The restaurant opened at nine. The bar was empty except for Domingo. His white linen jacket with its golden epaulets accentuated the wiriness of his shoulders. A nervous and erratic bull from Córdoba had slammed the barman's head against the boards sixteen years before, ending his fighting career at the age of twenty. I'd seen the photographs. Domingo was proud of them. They were a link with a more noble past. And since I could understand the loneliness of a man living in a world of complete silence, I had asked to see them again, giving him the pleasure of explanation.

I mouthed the Spanish greeting I'd learned, pointing through the open doors at the tiled patio. Parasols shaded the wickerwork tables and chairs. "A Pimms," I added in English. I waited at the bar, watching Domingo's flamboyant generosity with the bottle, the razor-thin parings of cucumber, the crown of mint and borage. I carried the tall frosted glass to the table at the far end of the patio. There was a glimpse of the Atlantic through the archway, a strip of silver beyond the fat green pine trees. I closed my eyes for a moment, savoring the scented warmth that clung to the walls of the patio. The voice behind me was familiar, the vowel sounds unmistakably Canadian.

"I guess I don't have to ask what brings *you* out so early this evening!"

I didn't even bother to turn my head. "For one thing it could have been lack of a hot bath."

Wolfie Field lowered himself into the spare chair. Eight consecutive years spent living in the sun had bleached out his thinning hair and given his scalp and the rest of his body a boot-polish tan. Wolfie had the mobile face of an actor, shrewd bloodhound eyes and a small paunch he concealed under well-cut trousers. He dressed entirely in white, May through September. Wolfie had headed the Scotland Yard list of wanted con men for three successive years without an arrest or conviction. I'd known him since 1962, the year he arrived in Europe, an adversary who neither asked for nor offered a deal. In 1966 an Interpol circular described Wolfie as a "traveling thief believed to be no longer operational." Scotland Yard had been less charitable. It was another four years before C.R.O. added the Canadian's file to the roster of rogues who were no longer gainfully employed at their trade.

Wolfie tilted his chair back and lit one of his cheroots. "I hear you changed your car."

"That's right," I admitted. A cop gets a kind of proprietary interest in the people he hunts. In Wolfie's case my interest was doubly strong. He'd outsmarted me over a considerable period of time, always playing the rules, and then finally disappearing. A couple of years ago somebody on the Fraud Squad had mentioned that Wolfie had bought a club in Spain. I squirreled away the information, forgetting it during the long winter that preceded my premature retirement. The Zaleski affair had kept me in England, the case dragging on into the summer recess. I was off the Force by then, no more than a witness for the prosecution. Drake took over the case. The Knight in Shining Armor cleaning up someone else's shit. I could have told him that Gerber would fight every inch of the way. We had a hung jury, a no-trial and an attempt to nobble a juror. It was October before Judge Collins did the country the favor of removing Gerber for the next fifteen years.

I spent that winter on the houseboat, listening to Vivaldi and being sorry for myself. There was no one really to kid me out of it. I spent days on end shuffling through travel folders. I didn't know where to go. All I was sure of was that I wanted to be out of England. Suddenly I remembered Wolfie Field. The idea seemed a good one. There would be sunshine and the chance to chew the fat with an old opponent, neither of us any longer a threat to the other. So I made my reservation and turned up in Las Ventas. After the first cautious sparring we achieved a sort of cut-and-thrust camaraderie.

I chewed on a sprig of mint and cocked my head sideways. "You ever thought about back-combing your hair, Wolfie?"

He fingered his scalp suspiciously. "How do you mean, back-combing my hair?" he demanded.

"It's what they do when it's thin," I explained. Wolfie's swan song, the final score that had allowed him to retire, had passed into criminal folklore. He'd made it with a broken-nosed Australian, familiarly known as "Petty Sid." They'd taken a non-protected Vegas gambler for half a million dollars in a racetrack swindle staged at Delmar. But as Wolfie always asserted loudly, it's impossible to beat an honest man at the con.

He glanced down at his fingertips as if the last of his hair was sticking to them.

"Dont' be smart," he said mildly. "Hey, there was someone looking for you this evening."

I spat out the chewed piece of mint. "He found me."

"I know all three of them," Field said smugly. The barman brought Wolfie's favorite tipple, champagne and orange juice, chilled and served in a silver goblet. Field drew hard on his cheroot and considered the end. "All three," he repeated.

"Congratulations," I said. There was a pattern about these conversations with Wolfie. The fancy footwork at the beginning was an essential.

He turned his wrist. He runs to expensive jewelry. His coin-thin Leuba watch had a sapphire crystal.

"Twenty after eight," he observed. "They shouldn't be long. Giselle's always punctual."

"Giselle?" I said.

He chased cigar smoke with a gulp from his goblet. "Giselle Dale."

A shred of mint was still lodged in my teeth. I dug it out with a pick. "Look, I appreciate your all round knowledge but let's get something straight. A woman left some things in the car I happen to be driving. The Garage Central gave her friend my name and I suppose, my address. He collected her property and suggested that we all have a drink later. As far as I'm aware there's neither mystery nor intrigue and that grin's getting on my nerves."

His expression sobered. "I know you, Raven. I wouldn't get any ideas about this chick if I were you. This one will nail your arse to the ground. Take my word for it; you'd be out of your league. In any case, she's part of a threesome."

I could hardly be described as a prude, yet the idea offended me. "How do you mean, a threesome?" I demanded.

He winked. "You'd better watch it; your eyes just crossed. A threesome's when you all love one another and there's no place in grandma's bed for a stranger."

I did my best to ignore his leer. "What else do you know about them?"

"It never fails, does it?" he said, putting the goblet down and shaking his head at me. "You just can't help yourself. It's a disease, like cholera. I really believe that if John the Baptist walked through that door you'd ask him if he could identify himself. Okay. They're in the film business and they're making a documentary about Pablo Beltrán."

I knew the name of course. There's a branch of journalism dedicated to publicizing the antics of the rich and

notorious. Beltrán happened to be both and it was difficult
to get away from the fact. His face stared from hoardings,
a tea cozy on his bald head, advertising some product he'd
given his name to. You read about him in the glossy art
reviews, the gossip columns. He was the archpriest of sur-
realism and a self-confessed genius. Whatever he said on
the subject of art was repeated with reverence. His forays
into finance were as successful as his painting. Whatever
he did was to shock the bourgeoisie. He once gave a ten
minute lecture in Carnegie Hall, defying gravity by sus-
pending himself upside down from a pair of gymnast's
rings. A shrewd Andalusian, his name was synonymous
with success. He was well over seventy and allegedly re-
juvenated by the use of Rumanian gland extracts. The pictures I'd seen of him showed a head like Borgia, no neck,
a big nose and eyes like horse chestnuts. He had a wife
called Dolores who was forty years younger.

"Now that *really* impresses me," I said. "I wouldn't
have thought Beltrán was the sort of man who needs publicity."

"Don't be righteous," he said. "Beltrán always needs
publicity. Especially for his Happenings."

It's a word I've never really understood but the dig
about righteousness kept me on my guard.

"I thought he lived in Madrid or New York."

"He does. He's a millionaire." There was a hint of
reproach in his tone for my ignorance. "And he happens
to have been born in a cow shed about fourteen miles from
here. That's his real home. Not the cow shed but a converted convent. That's where he paints."

"Yes, well," I said. "I never realized the extent of your
interest in the arts."

"Bullshit," he said. He looked at the end of his dead
cheroot. "You know you're out of touch, Raven. You've
been too long putting on those false beards, jingling the
handcuffs and locking people up. You've got to move with
the times, old man."

"I think you're a psychopath," I said steadily. "All these unjustified swings from gloom to gaiety. And vice versa. Let's get back to your friends. You mean Beltrán has actually hired them to do a documentary?"

"I didn't say that," he objected, pushing the flat of his hand at me. "What I said was they're making a documentary. Pablo Beltrán happens to be Franco's answer to all those commie painters like Miró and Picasso."

I beat my palms in applause. "Very good, Wolfie. Very good indeed. I'm impressed again."

He ignored the interruption. "People who left the country. So when a bunch of talented kids want to put the Maestro on film, he's hardly likely to refuse. Especially when it doesn't cost him anything. Try to understand, dunderhead. This is good for Spain. So good that the Minister for Information and Tourism himself is attending."

"And when is all this taking place?"

He was looking beyond me, his eyes on the bar. "You'll know. Behave yourself and I just might take you. On your feet, they're here."

He was a great one for the small courtesies and seemed to assume that other people's habits were less refined than his own. In fact in this mood he was a bloody bore. He walked toward the girl standing in the doorway, his arms stretched wide.

"Giselle, baby!"

I couldn't see her properly. The lower part of her face was half-hidden by Wolfie's shoulder. But her eyes were enormous and appeared to be fixed on me with an intensity that was almost hypnotic. She wriggled out of Wolfie's embrace and took Abbott's arm in a sort of sisterly hug. He'd touched up his eye shadow and was elegant in pink linen slacks and a Byronesque shirt.

"This is Mr. Raven, honey," he said in his well-bred voice. "Giselle Dale."

"How are you?" I said. Dale or Degenhardt, she was

more than just attractive; she was charming, managing the first blush I'd seen in a long while.

"I guess I have an apology to make, Mr. Raven. I'm sorry to have put you to so much trouble."

"There's no trouble at all," I assured her. She was wearing a black silk blouse buttoned low to reveal firm, high breasts, patent leather shoes and black velvet trousers molding her long slim legs. Her only jewelry was a simple watch on a strap. "A passport's a bad thing to lose. I did it once. I still start to shake when I think about it."

She gave me her hand. Her grip was firm and friendly. There was a gap between her front teeth and I tried to remember what it was supposed to denote.

"I don't usually lose things," she smiled. "Only Jerry's been away in Madrid and things here have been hectic."

Abbott rolled his eyes theatrically. "Five days away and they all start copping out!"

"I understand you're in the film business?" I said politely. She didn't have the chance to reply. We were standing in the entrance to the bar. A foursome in tennis clothes climbed onto the saddle stools. I recognized the two men and the girls as neighbors from one of the bungalows — Danes. Wolfie wrapped an arm around Giselle and Abbott and led them back to our table. She put herself between Wolfie and me. I held my lighter ready as she searched in her purse for cigarettes. I nodded at the pack of Sullivan Powells.

"You're the first person in real life I ever saw smoking those things. I don't suppose you ever read a book called *Raffles?*"

The gas ignited and her fingers touched my wrist very lightly. "E. W. Hornung. 'Raffles, the Gentleman Cracksman.' I grew up on it. My mother was English. Raffles smoked Sullivan Powells, that's right. And you're the first person other than my mother who ever remarked on it."

It was a cozy start and one that didn't seem to be doing

too much for Wolfie. He filled the two spare goblets from the silver jug. Wolfie expects his guests to approve his choice of food and drink.

"Well, I'm glad you people have met," he said sarcastically. "You know how long I know this guy?"

She was no more than inches away from me and I recognized the scent. It was the only one I *could* recognize, Estée Lauder. It tripped an old, old memory of a slender blonde in an Austrian ski lodge, pale and withdrawn, a challenge to my own loneliness. It had taken me six miserable months to realize that Cathy Stone's ethereal aloofness derived from shooting up a bag of smack a day. She was the first real junkie I had ever been in contact with and the shock almost demoralized me. I had to use everything I knew to get her on the Home Office list of registered drug addicts. A little blackmail, lies, appeals under the Old Pals Act. But it took her out of the hands of the dealers — or that's what it was supposed to do. She moved in with me on the houseboat. She was alone most of the day with the seagulls while I went through the motions of being a cop. The faintest whisper of what was going on in the right quarter and I'd have been off the Force. But nobody came near and I was convinced that we loved one another.

"Yes," said Wolfie. "I know him a long, long time. Right?"

"Right," I said. I'd no idea what was coming. I could only play it by ear.

"Eight years we've been friends," said Wolfie. "Well maybe 'friends' isn't the right word. The truth is we used to play hide-and-seek in the good old days."

Giselle's head turned toward me, her hair swinging. *"Hide-and-seek?"*

Wolfie's eyes crinkled maliciously. "He used to be a cop."

I should have known, of course. Wolfie was never reticent about his past. In fact he seemed to relish the subject and he was certainly a good raconteur. If anyone proved embarrassed it wasn't Wolfie.

Abbott gave a sort of choked giggle but his smoke blue gaze was thoughtful. "Do tell," he said lightly.

Wolfie Field stretched his legs and looked at a point somewhere over my head. There was no one else in the patio and the Danes were too pleased with their own company to worry about us.

I shrugged. "There's nothing to tell. I retired a year ago."

Giselle's chair scraped back. She wasn't wearing a bra and the silk blouse showed the unbound movements of her breasts.

"A detective-inspector, no less," said Wolfie. "They say that the underworld took up a collection to send him out of the country."

"It's a lie," I said sourly. "I only wish it were true, the prices you charge."

Wolfie went on, his expression indulgent. "Yessir, he was a real pain in the arse, one of these persistent sons-abitches who never gives up. I'll tell you something. I can remember this joker sitting in a tree for seven hours waiting for me to come out of a house."

It was no exaggeration. But what he didn't say was that it rained for most of the time and that in any case he'd left the house the previous day.

"Yes, well, that's history," I said. "And your friends aren't going to be interested in it."

"On the contrary," said Giselle. Her eyes had the glossy blackness of asphalt. "We're agog. I know Wolfie tends to pad out his scripts but this one sounds fascinating."

Something clicked in my mind. "I get the impression that you people knew one another before. You and Wolfie, I mean. Is that right?"

"Last year in Marienbad," said Wolfie.

"Very funny," I answered, cocking an eye at him.

"What's funny?" he demanded. He was oddly on edge.

21

"I happen to have a kidney condition and the kids were filming there."

"Tell me more about your filming," I asked.

She wriggled her nose. "There's not much to tell. We're a very small company doing specialized work."

Abbott took over. "We're using the medium to record the life-styles of people we believe to be geniuses. I'm sorry about the language but it's the only way I can put it."

I juggled my hands. "I can follow. Wolfie said you're working with Beltrán. I'd have described him more as show business though."

She mashed her cigarette in the ashtray. Her eyes were cool when she raised them. "Just how much do you know about Pablo Beltrán, Mr. Raven?"

"Only what I've read," I answered. I had a strong feeling that I was about to be put down.

"Only what you've read," she said in an aloof voice. "Then allow me to suggest something. Pablo Beltrán is as great a genius as Picasso was. The difference between them is that Beltrán's still alive and painting. What we hope to do is put the real man on film. Not just the artist but the man himself with all his human failings. All the lechery, selfishness and the kitsch. And if you don't admit those, Mr. Raven, it's impossible to appreciate the genius."

It sounded impressive but I had a sneaking feeling that she had made the same speech before.

"You're probably right," I admitted.

Abbott glanced at his watch. "We'd better go in," he suggested.

She gathered her things together and gave me her peculiar smile. "It was nice talking with you, Mr. Raven. I hope we meet again."

I stood as she walked away, her hand tucked under Abbott's arm.

"Well now," said Wolfie, dropping back into his chair.

"You blew that one for sure."

He'd been a boat rider for the first five years of his professional career. A Texan oilman in the Bahamas had listened to Wolfie's pitch for as much time as it took to down half a bottle of bourbon. Then he'd delivered his verdict in the shape of a round-arm swing that knocked the Canadian off his stool. Expert bridgework had repaired the damage to Wolfie's teeth but his nose had never been quite the same. I looked at it now with distaste.

"Why is it that you're always trying to score points off me? Do you fancy the girl yourself or what?"

"Hold it!" he said, shooting up his hand. "What are we doing here, putting the blame on *me*? I thought I was doing you a big favor with the Bow Street Runner bit. They lapped it up."

"You're dishonest," I said. "And devious. And unfriendly."

"All of those," he said cheerfully. "And I recognize a mark when I see one. That chick's got you going."

"Bollix," I answered. "She's got a certain manner, I'll admit. You know, a stretch on the Moor might have sweetened your character. I'll never know why I didn't slam you in the bucket."

"I'll tell you why," he said drily. "You never had the chance."

He had the nose of a fox and it was a lot easier to let him think what he wanted with reservations about what *you* thought he thought.

"Am I to understand that Giselle Dale means nothing at all in your life?" I demanded.

He shook his head. "Don't keep putting words in my mouth. All I'm trying to do is stop you from making a fool of yourself. Why don't you get out on the beach and meet some real people. I'm told there's a girl from Hamburg who makes it on a surfboard."

"You're dirty-minded as well," I retorted. The drink was working in my head and my boredom was gone.

"Where do these people live, anyway?"

He sighted along a fresh stogie. "A few miles out of town, a place called Villa Florida. It's on a bluff overlooking the ocean but they don't appreciate chance callers."

He was looking through the arch and beyond the trees. The smoke-smudge on the horizon was a freighter on its way to Cádiz.

"You're been to their house, of course?" It was illogical that the thought should disturb me but it did.

"Sure thing," he said easily. "I told you, Giselle and I are old friends. Here, try some of this. They call it Buck's Fizz."

I covered the top of my glass with my hand. "I don't like it. Too many fucking bubbles."

He eyed me thoughtfully. "They're good for your heartburn. Where are you going now?"

I was on my feet. "To eat. I might see you later."

I chose a table well away from Giselle and Abbott. They made no further sign of recognition but a couple of times I looked up and found her watching me. The food at Las Ventas was good but the accent was on fish. The chef came from Galicia. Tonight's offering was some sort of stew made of clams, peppers and dried cod. I left most of it. I refused the coffee, signed the bill and went down the steps to the edge of the pool. The boy had been round, picking up wet towels and folding the parasols. It was still light though the sun was long gone. Swallows were swooping low over the surface of the water. I sat on the wall staring out to sea. I couldn't get the memory of Giselle's face out of my mind, the wide hypnotic stare that drained without offering anything in return. There was a lie about her somewhere and I was determined to put my finger on it. The Beltrán business was hardly likely to be contrived. If the Spanish authorities were involved Abbott and company would have had to produce credentials. Maybe Giselle Dale was her professional name. It certainly sounded better than Gail Degenhardt. The prospect of finding out excited me. It wasn't a question of right or wrong, of morals. I didn't really care whether or not she was breaking the law. In any case it was no longer my business. This was something personal. There was a chemistry about her, an antagonism, that made me want to dominate her. One way or another, to make her aware of me as a man.

It was twenty-five to eleven when they came out of the restaurant. I kept well out of sight. She was talking animatedly as the green Peugeot pulled away with Abbott driving. I walked back through the trees to the bungalow and changed into jeans, a cotton shirt and sneakers. If I'd had any sense I'd have gone to bed. I backed the Seat out of the carport and drove down to the coastal highway. The stars were out and there was a distant sliver of moon hanging over the dark ocean. The filling station at the crossroads was open. I touched the horn. An attendant in overalls emerged from the lighted office carrying a transistor. He put the set on the ground as he milked the pump, listening to the blare of flamenco music. He was in his forties with a fat indifferent face. I found the money needed and added a few pesetas for the information I wanted.

"Por favor, la Villa Florida?"

He wiped the fuel cap with a rag and nodded in the direction I was pointed.

"Ocho kilometros. Un camino privado a izquierdo!"

That much I understood. Eight kilometers. A private road to the left. I nodded my thanks and released the hand brake. The empty highway followed stretches of bone white beach where black rollers broke on the sand leaving fringes of bubbling foam. I scratched involuntarily, thinking of the jellyfish out there, floating in the warm water, shapeless and poisonous. I kept an eye on the odometer. Six kilometers, seven, eight. It was the beginning of bull-breeding country and the right-hand side of the highway was heavily wired. An unbroken stretch of pasture vanished into the darkness. I changed down to low gear, letting the small car creep toward the signpost that pointed down a sandy lane. The beach ended suddenly, a line of trees marking the headland. I cut my lights, turning onto the lane and driving as far as a gate in a stone wall. I pulled off the lane into the trees and cut the motor. The only sound was the crash of waves below. I locked the car and took my bearings. The house lay somewhere in front of me. The greens were black in the moonlight, the shadows sharply defined. I closed the gate behind me and started walking. It was warm but cold fingers seemed to touch my back. I've never been able to understand when people make a clear-cut difference between fear and courage. For me they run hand in hand. I only know that I think too much to be brave. I kept away from the lane, climbing in and out of the deep arroyos that gouged the headland, trampling the fleshy mesembryanthemum. Oleander branches clutched at me stickily and I knew that what I was doing was stupid. There was a glow in the sky ahead, a couple of hundred yards away. I squatted down and chanced a cigarette. The smoke blew back in my face and I continued. I tried to relax, telling myself I was as good at this game as the next. A thief and a cop have much in common. They use the same skills, have the same pragmatic approach to the matter in hand. In fact, the hard-nosed veterans in outfits like the Flying Squad actually grow to look like and act like villains. They patronize the same bars and tailors, talk out of the sides of their mouths and generally behave like hoodlums. So much so that the public often takes one for the other.

I pushed the cigarette butt into the soft dirt and scrambled out of the last arroyo. A screen of pine trees hid a white two-story building with deep windows cut into thick walls. There were no lights showing inside. The glow in the sky I had seen came from the far side of the house. The green Peugeot was parked in front of the entrance porch. The villa was built on the point of the headland. Beds of unkempt carnations and cannas straggled between the walls of the house and the pines. I could hear the sound of music. I edged toward it, past the garbage can outside the kitchen window to the end wall. A shaft of light extended as far as the bushes that fringed the bluff. The rest of the garden was in darkness.

I ducked low, made the short dash to the cannas and crouched behind the saber-edged leaves. The ground was dry and caked. Things rustled close to my face. It was only two weeks since I'd seen my first scorpion and I couldn't get it out of my mind. It was three inches long, rusty brown in color, with a terminal sting like a whip. I parted the long stems and raised my head cautiously. I had a clear view of the rear of the house. The light came from a lamp hanging over the tiled terrace. There was a small pool and Giselle was lying by the side of it on a nest of cushions. She was wearing a yellow beach wrap and nothing under it. Her brown thighs and naked buttocks were clearly exposed. She was lying with her face turned upward, her eyes hidden in the crook of her elbow. Abbott was sprawling beside her, his shoulders still wet from the pool. Another man was squatting near them, head down, long straight black hair hanging in front of his face. A tape machine on a nearby chair was playing Nilsson. The three of them were completely immobile, like figures on a frieze, intent on the music.

A shift of breeze brought the unmistakable bonfire odor of hash to my nose. By craning a little I could see the long-stemmed pipe dangling in Abbott's fingers. I shifted my eyes back to Giselle. The realization that she was naked under the wrap gave me an odd sense of outrage. The music stopped abruptly, releasing the trio from its spell. Abbott rapped the pipe on the tiles and scattered the ashes with his bare foot. The other man raised his head, stretching his arms like a diver about to take off. His wedge-shaped face was cut in flat planes with black, barred eyebrows over an aquiline nose. His skin was the color of an autumn maple leaf. It was easy to imagine him in an eagle-feather headdress with a tomahawk in his hand. Abbott reached across and pulled Giselle's elbow away from her eyes.

The sound of his chiding voice drifted out into the warm scented night. "Secrets! You're not supposed to have secrets! You're going to make Lance and me jealous. Isn't she, Lance?"

The Red Indian rocked on his heels. I could see the brilliance of his teeth. His voice was a nasal drawl.

"Don't even *talk* about it! It isn't drink that's the curse of the redskin. It's the feeling of being an outcast."

"Send me a letter about it," she said shortly. She shaded her eyes from the fierceness of the lamp, looking up at Abbott. "How much of that stuff's left, lover?"

He wriggled a shoulder. "Enough. Why?"

"Stoke the fire," she ordered. "I've just made a decision."

Abbott went into the house. He came back rubbing something between his palms. He filled the pipe and passed it to Giselle. Lance was rocking, his arms around his knees. Abbott reversed the tape and the music started again. I could see Giselle's lips moving but her voice was drowned out. I crawled out of the cannas and worked my way back as far as the kitchen window. An inside door was open and I could see furniture in the room beyond, French windows and the gleam of the pool. Lance and Abbott were out of sight but I had a clear view of the woman. She was still talking. I leaned my weight against the kitchen door but the spring lock was fastened. My palms were sweating and I wiped them on my jeans and moved along the wall. The interior of the station wagon still smelled of Estée Lauder. I felt in the glove compartment. The only thing it held was a week-old parking stub from Cádiz Municipal Airport. The music was a blur of sound without melody. I stood there irresolute, the seconds stretching. The sensible thing to do was make tracks for my car, drive home and go to bed. This is what I reasoned but I'd no intention of doing it. The memory of Giselle's knowing smile somehow fortified my decision. What the hell *was* all this? I asked myself. A couple of fags and their little playmate, that's what. And she somewhat dubious to say the least. I climbed the two steps to the porch. The front door was unlocked. I followed my nose around it. There was some expensive looking movie equipment stacked in the hallway and enough light for me to see the stenciling on the cans of film: VIDEOART LTD. 55 DOVER ST. W.1

I shut the front door quietly and stood there with the entire house pressing in on me. My nose itched and my breathing was loud. A pile of damp, beach clothing was draped across the banisters on my left. I groped my way along the wall to the room I'd seen through the kitchen window. The terrace lamp threw sufficient back light. I could see newspapers strewn across the floor, a backgammon board on a table, a balloon with lipsticked eyes and mouth gently bobbing in the fireplace. I tiptoed across to an open window. Giselle was flat on the cushions, her wrap open to her navel. Lance was sitting by her feet; Abbott was somewhere out of sight. The tape was still playing but I could hear what she said.

"How do you mean, the Hearst girl?"

Lance's voice was smug and superior. "You know exactly what I mean, darling. Total commitment is what I mean."

She answered, enunciating very clearly. "Do I look like an idiot?"

Lance sounded surprised. "What's that got to do with it?"

She came up on an elbow. "You see! You don't know what's going on! It's all those mixed-up genes and the war drums playing in your head. I'll tell you about Hearst. She's a stupid little brat who thinks she's in *Bonnie and Clyde*."

I edged nearer the open window. I still couldn't see Abbott. Lance was holding the long-stemmed pipe, cupping the bowl with his hands as he inhaled. He offered it to Giselle, his face malicious.

"My, *my*, Miss Melissa!" he said in a bayou accent. His voice reverted to normal. "When the paddy wagon calls, the good girls go with the bad, remember."

She released the smoke reluctantly. "I'm hardly likely to forgot it. It's a screwed up world but we have to keep the faith."

He rolled over, letting one foot dangle in the water. "You're so fucking sure of yourself. You're Barnum and Bailey but you scare me at times."

She rapped the empty bowl on the tiles and scattered the ashes as Abbott had done. "Do tell, pray!"

He studied the ripples spreading across the surface of the water before he replied.

"Well this guy at the country club for instance. An ex-cop no less. How the fuck can you be sure that he didn't look at that passport?"

"I can't," she said in a level voice. "That's why we're going to find out."

"*We*," he repeated sarcastically, drying his toes with fastidious care. "Mata Hari leaves her device in the bidet and suddenly it's everyone go look for it. I've put a lot into this, Giselle, baby."

Her diction was even clearer than before. "We've *all* put a lot into it. But yours is only money. Jerry and I blew our careers."

"Big *freak-out!*" he jibed. "A silly old news cameraman and the fourth grade history teacher. You can huff and puff just as much as you like but you don't impress me, baby. *You're* the one who left that fucking passport in the car, not me."

She made a long humming sound and then laughed. "Let me remind you of something, buster. I had to hustle a man with bad breath to get you out of the morals charge in Hamburg. Latvian sailors, indeed! I'll tell you what you are, Lancey, sweetheart. You're just a Navaho fag who happens to own a hole in the ground in New Mexico. So oil comes out of the hole and that is supposed to make you something very, very special. Some kind of fucking Mahatma. The reality is that you are a nothing.''

The way she said it would have moved me to the kind of behavior best left to insulted truck drivers. Then, incredibly, I heard a cistern flush somewhere upstairs. I'd taken it for granted that Abbott was out on the terrace but the bastard was actually in the house. Any moment now and he'd be starting back down the stairs. I gauged the distance from the window to the open kitchen door. With any sort of luck I could make it and hide before he reached the hallway. Then a door slammed overhead and the house was quiet again. I took another look through the window. Lance was sitting up stiffly, arms folded across his chest, looking across the pool.

Giselle rose, bent and kissed him lightly on the cheek. ''Noble savage in repose.''

He looked up at her, baring his teeth in a forced smile. ''You're adorable. I just wish I had your scalp on my belt.''

She ran her fingers down his jawline. ''Don't worry about a thing, Lance, baby. Mamma has everything under control.''

He made a sour face and collected his towel. She was already halfway across the terrace to the French windows. If I tried for the kitchen now I'd meet her head-on. There was a big square sofa at the end of the room. I went down behind it with the smell of dust in my nose. The ceiling darkened as the terrace lamp was extinguished. I heard her clogs on the staircase, then Lance shutting the French windows. The front door was bolted. Someone started running a bath. Bedroom lights shafted across the pool, illuminating the tangle of bushes on the point of the headland. A radio belted out monotonous rock.

I came up from behind the sofa very cautiously. The

time to leave was now. They were too busy to notice the back door open or closed. I let myself out silently and ran for the shadows.

It was after midnight when I reached the club but the bar was still crowded. The lights were on in Wolfie's apartment. The Canadian was the one man likely to appreciate the situation but I'd no intention of confiding in him. For one thing there was all this crap about Marienbad — the suggestion that he had prior claims on the girl, an intimacy with her from which I was excluded. I drove down to the bungalow, parked and lit a cigarette. The moon was high, warm and yellow — completely different than the cold silver circle I was accustomed to. I took my cigarette to the springy grass and walked there, trying to get my thoughts in order. The fact that was foremost in my mind was that I'd just risked making the biggest kind of bloody fool of myself. I could so easily have been caught prowling around in somebody else's house without a prayer of an excuse. And for what? I asked myself. Well, in the first place there was the matter of a hunch. A lot of what I'd seen and heard tonight I didn't understand but one thing was for sure, VideoArt Ltd. was deeply disturbed by the possibility of my having seen the Gail Degenhardt passport. It was conceivable that another one existed in the name of Giselle Dale. Wolfie was supposed to have met her in Czechoslovakia and he'd introduced her as Dale. Apart from that there was nothing I could put my finger on. The hash was unimportant. The findings of the Boothby Commission on the use of cannabis held that one adult in ten living in London had tried the drug in one form or another. I smoked, myself, when the time and company were right. And there was no law against a girl living with a couple of queers. As a matter of fact, there were circles where it would have been felt a natural and sensible arrangement.

I yawned and put my foot on the cigarette stub. Bed looked good and, mercifully, there were no mosquitoes. I lay in the darkness, hands locked behind my head, my nose just free of the one sheet that covered me. Sleep was evasive, disturbed by the memory of a woman I didn't even know. The archtype of the kind of woman I usually avoided. Yet the mere thought of her set the adrenalin racing. I told myself that I was too old, too battered, to fall into the same trap twice. Yet I knew that I was very near it.

To scatter love on the ocean and accept disaster. Cathy had said it seven long years before. Cathy, with the gleaming body smelling mysteriously of cloves. Cathy, whose courage was never quite enough to fight her heroin habit, who laughed at my fury when the gulls shit on the deck of the houseboat. Sweet warm Cathy who finally swallowed thirty-six barbiturate tablets because I'd never learned to give the love she needed.

3

I AWOKE at seven-thirty as I'd been doing for the past eighteen years. Neither booze, women nor worry seem to break the habit. I swung myself out of bed and sat scratching the jellyfish stings. It would be another hour before the maids brought my breakfast. I pulled on my swimtrunks and went outside. The ants were still busy in the grass. The bloody things never seemed to sleep.

I could see a couple of fishing boats chugging across the placid Atlantic toward Las Ventas. Early sunshine warmed the pines but there was no birdsong. I missed birdsong but there was none in this country and I understood why. Anything feathered that sang or flew was either trapped or shot.

The shutters were closed in the neighboring bungalow. A German couple had been there for three weeks. The woman owned a chain of sex shops and her husband danced the tango. He'd given up introducing himself but he still nodded briskly whenever we met. I stepped out onto the grass and started throwing my arms about vigorously, breathing in deeply till my lungs protested. A few minutes of it were quite enough. *Mens sana* etc., a spin-off from a public school education together with a revulsion to sleeping in the same room with anything male and a cast-iron stomach.

I showered and shaved, choosing a blue short-sleeved shirt to go with the flared denims. Sweeny Todd was going to bang on about my hair when I got back to London. "All these sun-bleach streaks! And the ends! And too *long*, Mr. Raven!" But I wasn't about to trust the crowning glory to some village barber. I opened the windows wide and sat under the trellis-work, thumbing through a battered police notebook. A felt pen had obliterated most of the telephone numbers. The ex-directory entries with the coded circuits, the series of digits that had linked me with the more esoteric law-enforcement agencies. I'd used any help I could get in the past, only eschewing informers. It seemed to me that men who were ready to rat on their own kind weren't to be trusted.

I found the number I was looking for under "S." Soo, Jerry. I marked the page, tapped a Ducados from the pack and left it on the table. I've always been good at the small self-disciplining exercises. No smoking before breakfast, no spirits till after seven in the evening, clean socks and underwear twice a day if possible. As my father used to say, you never know when and where you might have to strip. It was my refusal to accept the other forms of discipline that had ultimately destroyed me as a cop. I was never able to give the blind obedience that's supposed to accompany a salute. Injunctions like "First carry out your order, then state your objection" seemed to me to be ridiculous. I supposed my whole life-style was an offense to discipline. Yet I *was* a good cop.

I dropped the dog-eared notebook in my pocket, thinking about Jerry Soo. "So solly Jelly," the only Hong Kong-born cop on the Metropolitan Police Force. Right now he'd be sitting up in his sixth-floor office at Scotland Yard, collating crime statistics. The incidence of Breaking and Entering per mile in the Royal Borough of Chelsea and Kensington, the swing in the three parks from Soliciting to Indecent Exposure. There'd be a package of egg sandwiches in Jerry's top right-hand drawer together with Brand's Catalogue of Valuable Postage Stamps. I'd been close enough to Jerry over the years to know that he'd do whatever I asked of him.

The click of wooden heels and the smell of coffee heralded the arrival of breakfast. I ate it on the terrace and smoked my first cigarette. I wanted to talk to Wolfie Field without him attaching too much importance to it. By the time I made my way past the club pool it was well after eleven. I closed my nostrils against the reek of suntan oil. A large man was floating on a rubber mattress reading *Der Spiegel*. Herr Graebner. I acted as if I hadn't seen him wave. The putting green in front of Wolfie's windows was pool-table smooth and edged with sand traps. Hot sun had dried the watered grass to a fast true surface. The two Colombian sisters were sitting on the terraced bank, reading. They were elegant creatures, like silk-clad leopards, in Pucci pants and headbands. An airplane crash in Brazil had widowed them jointly and they were in Spain looking for trouble of their own choosing. They were staying at the club but their base appeared to be Madrid, where, seemingly, they knew everyone.

A boy in a faded uniform was in a chair under a striped parasol. He selected an iron and a putter and handed them to me together with a ball.

I held up two fingers. "Two. *Dos balls*."

He rolled another ball across the grass. "You play with someone, Meester?"

There was a note of incredulity that I accepted without question. People always expect me to be alone. Waiters steer me automatically to a table for one, unable to credit that I just might be waiting for a guest. Barmen in discothèques offer me advice about the local female talent. I toed one of the balls into line and smacked it straight into the nearest sand trap. I stuffed the other ball in my hip pocket, winked at the boy and walked away. Hot sand poured into my sneakers as I scrambled down into the bunker. My ball was lodged under the lip of the bunker and unplayable. I pulled it back a yard and took a practice swing. An expected voice came from behind.

"I saw that, you cheating bounder!"

Wolfie was hanging out of his bedroom window, pointing. I completed my stroke. The ball struck the side of the sand trap and rolled back again.

"You're checking your swing," he bawled. "I told you that before and you're still doing it! Keep your eye on the ball!"

I shaded my eyes from the sun and walked a couple of yards toward the window. "I keep forgetting how much better you can do."

He drew back propping his elbows on the windowsill. "A hundred pesetas I'm on the green in one and sink it in two."

"Riveting." I said politely. "You're on."

He was down within seconds, dressed in freshly laundered chinos and an open-necked shirt. He took my iron from me, bent his tanned scalp and assessed the angle from the trap to the flag above. Then he swung the club and the ball soared cleanly. We climbed out of the bunker. The ball was lying three feet away from the hole. The Colombian sisters were watching closely. I gave him the putter and pulled the flag out of the hole. The ball rattled into the cup.

I gave him his money. "Brilliant. Now you can buy me a cup of coffee."

He swept a mock bow to the sisters and went up the bank with this hop-skip-and-a-jump he assumes in a good mood. The bar was empty, the tables decked with flowers, the windows open to the sea breeze. Wolfie dragged a chair back, stretched out his legs and lit a cheroot. His eyes were shrewd.

"Okay. What's on your mind!"

38

"Nothing," I said. "I was just taking a little exercise and meditating on God's infinite wisdom."

The coffee was Salvadorian Highland and came from that good store in Cádiz. Wolfie claimed that he lost money with every cup that was served.

"Bullshit," he said. "You're going to try to fuck me up. I can feel my feet curling."

I shook my head at him. "You're paranoid, that's your trouble."

He wagged a finger from side to side. "Look, Raven. You've been acting very strangely for the last few hours. What is your difficulty!"

"Difficulty!" I gave him the old charge room smile. Let Me Be Your Friend. You Can Rely On Me. "I was thinking about that party, the Beltrán Happening. I'd like to go."

"Well now," he said, opening his foxy eyes very wide. "There's one thing I forgot to tell you. The men are supposed to go dressed as women and vice versa. That lets you out. Your legs are terrible."

"I've seen yours," I reminded him sharply.

He sighted along his cheroot. "Giselle Dale's got you hooked, right!"

We considered one another like chess players. "Let's say I'm interested," I admitted. "*Intrigued*."

He spooned more sugar into his coffee. "Life's a funny thing."

"Yes," I said. "Life's a funny thing."

He rocked his chair with his leg. "It must be kind of confusing to you. I mean having had all that saluting and the superlatives. There you were, the hotshot inspector and suddenly, bam! You're out on your ear, hobnobbing with the likes of Wolfie Field. Terrible."

"I survive," I said shortly. The conversation wasn't taking the line I expected.

He nodded sagely. "Oh, you're a survivor, I'll give you that."

I put my cup down. The coffee had suddenly lost its savor. "I don't know that I appreciate your tone too much."

"Come on, now," he urged. "Let's not get into semantics and bad feeling. I happen to know it was either resign or your arse over there in London last year. I mean after the Gerber case."

I spaced my words very deliberately. "You are wrong. My arse, as you so delicately call it, has always been mine. You see I'm what the French call *integre*."

"Are you now," he replied. "Well ever since you've been here you've been bitching about the Police Force. Sharks, you said. All teeth and no brains."

I tilted the coffeepot, refilling my cup. "Ruthless and cannabalistic," I said. "Don't worry about it. The description applies to a lot of people."

"Don't look at me," he said comfortably. "I'm *supposed* to be like that, remember. We're talking about you. How about you, Raven?"

I raised a shoulder. "I don't know about me."

"Then I'll tell you," he said. "You've got what's called the cancer of compassion. You just can't manage that last kick in the balls. That's why you didn't last on the Force."

"Your friends are looking," I said. The Colombian sisters were at the bar, working on their first stingers. Both spoke excellent English and their hearing was sharp.

"Will there be any chance to see Beltrán's paintings at this affair?" I asked.

"A *chance*?" Wolfie choked on a chuckle and cleared his throat noisily. "You've got this all turned round, Raven. You're talking about the best con man since the Indiana Kid, the biggest show on earth. With the camera on him and a cabinet minister present there will be no way to avoid seeing those pictures. We'll have the whole production. The great lover's technique with the models involved, the value of each God damn brush stroke."

There was a loose hair in my nostril and I plucked it out. "You say that's where he paints? I mean in this converted convent?"

"That's right." He wiggled his fingers at the Colombians. *"They'll* be there, complaining about the champagne and talking about their platinum deposits. The Minister's a friend of theirs."

"But the paintings must be worth a fortune," I insisted. "Who lives in the house?"

"The servants," he said absently. "Beltrán only goes there a couple of times a year." He smiled and winked, his eyes on the younger of the two sisters. She turned her back on him deliberately. "Bitch," he muttered.

"Make no mistake," he continued. "When it comes to making money and keeping it, this character takes lessons from no one. The invitation list was closed two weeks ago but if you really want to go I'll try to fix it with Giselle."

The sun was high, filling the patio with light and warmth. "Did you ever marry?" I said suddenly.

He shook his head. "What makes you ask a thing like that?"

I worried the end of my nose where the hair had been. "I don't know. You don't feel you've missed anything?"

He half shut his eyes. "How about you?" he countered.

I didn't know how to answer. In fact I didn't know why I'd asked the question. I compromised by shrugging.

He rattled the change in his pockets. "If I gave you a straight, straight answer you wouldn't believe me, would you?"

"No," I admitted. I was thinking of my sister Frances with the kids at school and her husband lecturing to militant trouble-makers. Right now she'd probably be in the kitchen, fighting the endless battle with meals, her paints and easel up in the attic, forgotten, like her dreams. If that's what marriage was about I wanted no part of it.

Wolfie gave me one of those infuriating smiles of understanding. "You're a disturbed man, Raven. My advice is not to waste your time with women like Giselle Dale. You need company, better you settle for one of the Colombians. Now do you want to eat with me or not?''

I stood up. "No thanks. I'll get something in the village. I'll see you later.''

4

LUNCH WAS a plate of charcoal-grilled sardines and a pint of cold draft beer in a bar that had AQUI SÉ HABLA ESPAÑOL chalked across the window. It was the owner's reply to the neighboring establishments and their boasts of familiarity with English and German. I didn't hurry with my meal and it was after three when I paid my bill. It was siesta time and Las Ventas was sleeping. I'd learned that post offices in Spain handle no more than the dispatch of mail. Telephone and telegram services are housed in separate locations. A goat was cropping weeds in front of the Civil Guards Barracks. A sentry cradling a machine-gun lolled against the wall watching it. Over his head was the familiar red and yellow ensign and an engraved sign that said TODO POR LA PATRIA. I could see the row of iron cots through the dormitory windows. I'm one of those people who is scared out of his life by the sudden apparition of the gray green uniforms and patent leather hats. These jokers have a mindless dedication that terrifies me.

I climbed steps into the cool hallway of the telephone office. The house was old, the stone flags polished by generations of footsteps. I poked my head through an open door. A wax-faced man in a kind of bib was sitting behind a desk, a dial phone in front of him. Above his head was a photograph of the Generalissimo that must have dated back to the Civil War. There was a large fan in the ceiling and a booth the shape and size of a confessional. Hooked on the wall of the booth was an old-fashioned telephone.

"You quierro telefonar para London," I said.

The operator raised blank eyes, *"Para Dónde?"* he said through his noise.

"I'd rehearsed the phrase but it didn't sound right. I tried again. *"Londres?"*

"Ahhh —Londres!" There was a Sacred Heart emblem pinned on his chest. *"Qué numero?"* he asked suspiciously.

I gave him the exchange and number. He oozed over the desk, searching for the correct area code. Then he dialed and nodded.

"A la cabina. Habla!"

"Detective-Inspector Soo," said the voice.

"John Raven," I answered.

"John *who?"*

"Raven."

He made a clucking sound with·his tongue. "You must have the wrong number. This is New Scotlard Yard, extension five-five-o. Detective-Inspector Soo speaking."

The connection was good. I could hear the clatter of a telex in the background, the noise of traffic. It was typical that in spite of regulations and air conditioning, Soo would find a window to open. I moved my face nearer the mouthpiece.

"Here comes the magic word that changes you into Prince Charming. Bollix!"

"That is *definitely* John Raven," he replied. "They told me you were in Spain."

"I am," I said. "Can you talk or not?"

The phone went dead as his hand covered the microphone. Then he was back.

"Go ahead, John."

I took a look over my shoulder. The operator was picking his noise, absorbed in some religious newspaper. The fan had enormous blades like those on an old-fashioned airplane. The newspaper lifted with each revolution.

"I need some information," I told him. "Is the iron brain still working?" After years of false alarms, the National Police Computer was finally operative.

"I think so, yes. Whenever it feels in the mood."

"And can you get anywhere near it?"

"Absolutely. Rank and privilege, you know. What do you need?"

"Do you have a pencil and paper?"

His voice went tinny. "This conversation is being recorded automatically. Please state your name and address clearly."

"That is very funny," I said. "Now take these names and shove them through the mixer. Jerry Abbott. Gail Degenhardt. Giselle Dale." I still didn't know the Indian's surname. "They're all Americans. See what you can get for me."

His voice changed to a chop suey accent. "Mistah Laven lunning aftah Amellican guhls?"

"You're a natural," I said. "A fantastic sense of humor! A great act for a Masonic dinner! So what you do is check the *Companies Register* for an outfit called VideoArt Ltd., 55 Dover Street. Anything at all you can learn, okay?"

I held the receiver away from my ear as Soo's discordant whistle traveled a thousand miles. The tune was "Once in the Dear Dead Days Beyond Recall."

"Still having fun?" I asked pointedly.

"Eight hours a day," he replied. "And double fun for overtime. How about you?"

"Phenomenal," I answered. "I've discovered that I'm not a fisherman. How soon can you get back to me?"

There was a pause as he made his calculations. "A

couple of hours. What time is it now, four? How about six o'clock; that do?"

That would be seven, local time. There was no reason why I shouldn't take the call at the club. The lines were direct to the bungalows and metered. I gave him the number.

"I'd do the same for you, Jerry."

"I doubt it," he said and hung up on me.

It took the operator five minutes and several pieces of paper to determine how much I owed him. I found the money and walked out into strong sunlight. The village was still somnolent, flat on its back. The sentry, half-dozing, was watching the goat chew the edge off a loose poster. I made my way back down to the *embarcadero* and the parked Seat. Home again, I sat under the bamboo awning wondering what Soo would come up with. It was the moment for old friendships to pay off and Christ knows I had few of them. Soo and I had gone through police college together, each of us a misfit in his own particular fashion. The years separated us and then brought us together again. We were both still bachelors and when it came to the religion of law and order, profound agnostics.

I hauled my jeans down and inspected the worst of the jelly-fish stings. The blotches seemed to have faded under the lotion. Someone at the club had said that it took a week for the poison to disperse. Suddenly I heard a noise. A small noise but an unfamiliar one. It sounded like metal scraping on stone. I pulled my pants up quickly and eased myself out of the car. All I could hear now was the droning of the wasps congregating around the end of the hosepipe. I tiptoed along the sun-baked terrace as far as the windows. The maids always left the curtains closed to keep the interior cool. I heard the same noise again, this time from the front of the house.

"Who's there?" I yelled.

The umbrella pines swallowed the challenge. Nothing moved. The Graebners' white Mercedes glimmered through the trees. I ran around the end wall, skidding on the flagstones. Bugs droned among the bougainvillea. Everything was peaceful. I let myself into the bungalow, holding my nose till I opened some windows. The place stank of insecticide. There was a copy of yesterday's *Daily Telegraph* on the bedside table. I stripped to my shorts and lay down on the bed with the newspaper. The news from England was heart-warming. Muggings on the underground. Sex instruction for ten-year-olds. A woman prosecuted under the Race Relations Act for advertising for an English cook. It seemed that even an illegal immigrant had more rights than a native of Britain. No wonder that a man like Sir Oswald Mosley was a voluntary exile. I let the paper fall to the ground and dozed till the phone jangled. I grabbed the receiver. It was the operator from the International Exchange.

"Mr. Raven? One moment, please, I have a call for you from London."

I carried the phone to a table and back, collecting pen and paper. "Jerry? Go ahead, Jerry."

"Here it is," he said. "VideoArt Ltd. The address is that of the company secretary, Stuart Berman, solicitor. There's only one director, a United States citizen, Lance Deerwater Christian. According to the articles of association the company is engaged in public relations and was formed five months ago with a capital of a thousand pounds. Are you listening?"

"Agog," I said.

"Okay. The names you gave me: C.R.O. has no record of arrests or convictions on any of them. Here's what the Aliens Office has. Jerry Abbott and Gail Degenhardt, also United States citizens, arrived at Stansted Airport, October 5, 1974. They landed in a helicopter piloted by Lance Deerwater Christian."

I was having a job getting it down. Cathy had taught me the rudiments of shorthand but its use set up bad vibes.

"How about Giselle Dale?" I asked.

"There's no such person," said Soo. "Not according to the computer. I mean as an American citizen in England."

"Go on," I said. That was one question answered at least.

"VideoArt Ltd. is engaged in the dissemination of information dealing with worthwhile art forms."

"What's that supposed to mean?" I demanded.

"A three months' work permit is what it means. It's what they applied for and what they got. They took a furnished house in Hampstead and paid a year's rent. Lance Deerwater Christian signed the lease. There are no debts, no black marks and E. Division never heard of them. Shall I tell you about the helicopter, John?"

"You fuck around with me," I warned, "and I'll do you a lot of nastiness. And when you come to the name 'Christian' again, you can forget the Lance Deerwater bit."

He laughed. "He's got the right kind of pilot's license. With over a thousand hours' flying time. The chopper's registered in the name of the company and I checked with Stansted. It makes sense."

"*What* makes sense?" I demanded. He'd always been a clown but this was ridiculous.

"Well, it could be used for business. It's got a range of over six hundred miles without refueling, five seats, and does a hundred and forty miles an hour carrying a payload of more than a thousand kilos. It's German and called a BO one-o-five. Perfect for a bank job."

"What bank job are you talking about?"

His voice was dead straight. "Well, it could land on top of a Securicor van, for instance, lower its grappling irons and, away."

"Look," I said patiently. "Would you mind telling me when these people left the U. K. or doesn't your information stretch that far?"

"Sure," he said cheerfully. "They cleared Stansted on May twelfth, logged destination Le Bourget."

"Could they have hired the helicopter?" I asked.

"They could but they didn't," he said. "Lance Dee ... *Christian* bought it in Munich for nine hundred fifty thousand Deutsche marks. Get your pencil and work it out. This is a lot of money. Are you sure you know what you're doing, John?"

"No," I said. "I'm not sure. But thanks anyway. Let me know how much I owe for the call."

"It's on the house," he answered. "We look after our own, even the renegades. Keep in touch."

I swung my feet to the floor thinking "helicopter." A door opened in my mind and I remembered the parking stub I had found in the station wagon. Where likelier for a helicopter to be than Cádiz Municipal Airport? It was important to me to see it. Not that I didn't trust Soo. I just wanted to be sure of every piece of ice I was walking on. The scribble on the paper in my hand was barely decipherable. I threw it in the waste basket. Whatever I needed was locked in my head.

I put my clothes on again, made sure of the windows and shut the front door behind me. It was eight or ten degrees cooler outside. I walked round to the back of the house with the impression that I was being watched. The Graebners' Mercedes was gone so it wasn't them. I could see a dog on their terrace scavenging from an overturned garbage can. Nothing else. Yet the feeling persisted. It's a disturbing feeling that can come from seeing a vague shape in a car, a head turned in a doorway, the smell of a cigarette that shouldn't be there. But this time there was nothing. No more than the silent pine trees and the distant smack of tennis balls.

Cádiz Municipal Airport was a twenty-minute drive away. I stopped at the barrier and bought a parking ticket. Cars were drawn up in front of a single-story white building. Sunlight flashed on the windows of the control tower behind it. There were a couple of hangars off to the side on a baked dirt runway. Heat shimmered over the one strip of tarmac. The flight path was due south, out across the Bay of Cádiz. There was no commercial traffic. I could see the offices of a flying club. The few light planes on the ground were obviously privately owned. It was the sort of place for a family excursion. There was more breeze out here than in the city. Parents were drinking at the open-air bar while their children rampaged through the play area.

I strolled past the administration building. The two cops in the doorway paid me no heed, indifferent behind their smoked glasses. Security was negligible. I slipped round behind a fuel storage tank and walked toward the hangars. A mechanic was working on a Piper Cub with his back to me. I could see the helicopter in the open hangar behind him, squatting like a giant blue and black dragonfly with shining Plexiglas eyes. I could read the marking on the slender tail. D MDAF. The mechanic turned suddenly and we looked one another full in the face. I zipped my fly up and down and strolled back toward the cars. I was twenty yards away when I saw Wolfie's Volkswagen. The top was down, the convertible empty. I lit a cigarette and made my way across the hot cement to the Seat. Wolfie was waiting in the passenger seat. I climbed in beside him. He hung for a minute as if choosing his words. There was a look on his face that I remembered from years ago. It wasn't as much hostility as warning, the stage that in a dog means raised hackles and stiff legs. But his voice was quiet enough.

"I hope I'm not going to have a problem with you, Raven."

The car suddenly seemed very small for both of us. I leaned back as far as my legs would allow me. "You may well have, Wolfie, if you keep following me."

He nodded across at the hangar. "That thing belongs to the kids. I want to know what the fuck you're playing at."

I lowered the window and propped my elbow on it. There were grass stains — or what looked like them — across the front of his trousers.

50

"Was that you creeping around my bungalow this afternoon?" I asked him.

His nose thinned leaving a knuckle of white in the tan where it had been broken.

"Don't try to blow anything past *me*," he said in a tight voice. "I've got a right to know where you're at."

I held up a finger. "Don't talk to me about rights, Wolfie. I've got a good memory."

"Okay, Okay!" he said quickly. It was the actor's smile now, the quick warm smile that both explained and accepted. "Let's put it this way. You and I know one another a long time, right?"

"Right," I said cautiously. "So?"

He spread his hands. "So you're staying in my place as a guest and acting like a cop. It makes me nervous, Raven. It upsets me."

"I'm sorry about that," I answered. "Maybe you'd like me to pay my bill and leave."

"You could always do that," he agreed. Sweat was gathering in his scalp and his fingers were nervous. "But you won't. All I'm asking you to do is be reasonable. People around here respect me, Raven. All that old shit's forgotten."

"I'm delighted to hear it," I said. "We all need respect. Next question. Why am I out here looking at a two-hundred-thousand-pound helicopter?"

His face was sour. "Because there's a Dick Tracy peeping out of every fucking cop, that's why."

"Wrong," I said. "It's Sherlock Holmes. How well do you think you know these kids, as you call them?"

He looked at me sideways but one eye was enough to show his wariness.

"How well do I *think* I know them? I don't follow you, Raven."

"Then I'll try again," I said. "You've been at it as long as I have, Wolfie. We like to think we're men of the world. I'm going to put one question to you and I want a straight answer. Doesn't your nose tell you that there's something not quite right about your friends?''

He frowned, a schoolmaster confronted with doubts about his favorite pupils. Then his face cleared. "You almost had me going there! Okay, someone's told you they smoke the odd joint. They do but they're certainly not dealers.''

I pitched the butt through the window and watched it smolder. "No," I said finally. "I wouldn't think they're dealers.''

"Then *what?*" he insisted. He was sweating and obviously looking for a fight.

"Look, just take it easy," I said. "We're not going to get anywhere snarling at one another. What made you follow me here?''

His pale blue eyes wavered but only for a second. "Because I don't trust you, Raven. It's as simple as that. Just who the hell do you think you are, poking and prying. What is it with you; what are you out to prove?''

"I'm like you, Wolfie. Curious. No more, no less.''

His stretched face with its boot-polish tan gave him the look of one of those old tennis bums you see playing in minor tournaments for expenses and whatever else they can pick up.

"Don't tell me you're still working for the law!" he challenged.

"I couldn't buy a ticket to a traffic warden's dance," I assured him. "I'm John Raven, loosely described as of independent means, normally residing on a houseboat moored in Chelsea Reach and presently on holiday. And I don't like being followed.''

"You don't?" he said, shaking his head. "That's good from someone who was in the business. I think you're just a miserable son of a bitch who can't kick the old habits.''

He was smiling now but he meant it. Just the same we'd traded too many insults in the past for me to take offense.

"I'm going to put a simple question to you," I said.

"You've led what I'd call a fairly full life. How many straight people have you met who go around using double identification?"

"Double identification?" He repeated the words as if I'd spoken Chinese.

I nodded. "That's right. Tweedledee and Tweedledum."

He brushed at the stains on the front of his Levis. "Here we go with the nods and winks again. Just exactly what are you getting at, Raven?"

"Your playmates are what I'm getting at," I answered. "I've got an idea one of them is traveling on a phony passport. You know, one of those little numbers your pal Dutch Sam used to turn out, good for any country except the one it's supposed to come from."

"You're hallucinating," he said shortly and turned his head away.

"You know me better than that," I answered.

He shaved his cheekbone with a couple of fingers, his eyes intent on mine.

"Okay. Which one?"

"I've got an idea you know already," I said steadily. "Giselle Dale."

His frown hardened to a scowl. "What is this, one of your fucking hunches or do you go around inspecting people's passports?"

"One of the things she left in the car was a passport."

"So?" He licked his lips, then wiped his mouth on the back of his hand. "She's cashed checks with me."

"In the name of Giselle Dale?"

"You're damn right," he retorted. "And don't forget that I was with her in . . ."

"Marienbad." I finished it for him. "I'm sure it was all very exciting for you but it doesn't alter the fact that the lady has a passport in one name and an international driver's license in another. She's either Gail Degenhardt or she's Giselle Dale. She can't logically be both."

He wound the window up and down. "There just *has* to be a reason. I mean a legitimate reason. Maybe she was married. That's it. So she uses both names."

I wagged my head from side to side. "You don't change your name from Gail to Giselle when you marry, Wolfie. You'll have to do better than that."

He wiped his hands and felt in his pockets for his cheroot case. "I give up. What are you going to do about it, anyway?"

I answered him truthfully. "I'm not sure. A lot depends on you."

He shot me one of his oblique glances, too quickly done to read the expression in his eyes. "I'm not too sure I like the way this conversation's going. Why should it depend on me?"

I gave him a match for his smoke and lit my own cigarette. "Let's come at it from a different angle, Wolfie. You and I used to belong to the same sort of world. I suppose we still do. So I'm not about to tread on your corns if I can help it. Do I make myself clear?"

"No, you do not," he answered. "I don't know what the fuck you're talking about."

I blew smoke out into the clear air. "Then make yourself comfortable. Your friends are up to some sort of villainy. I'm convinced of it. Now I'll admit that it's no business of mine and that I shouldn't really worry about it. But I've been involved. To the point where I'm curious. And I'm worried about you. Let's call it for old-times' sake."

"Why should you be worried about me?" he demanded guardedly.

"I can't answer that one," I said. "It's just a feeling at the moment."

Some of the suspicion seemed to leave him. "You mean you're going to the police with this kind of shit?"

"I didn't say that, did I? What I said was that I was getting curious. Everyone else is doing his number, Wolfie. Why shouldn't I?''

He made a long humming noise before he answered. ''You're not really concerned with these people, are you, Raven? You're just sniffing around after me, aren't you? You want to know how I come into all this, right?''

''Partly right,'' I said. ''But your girl friend excites my imagination as well. I get the impression she thinks I'm sort of a clown.''

''I told you,'' he said, staring. ''You're a disturbed man. Let me lay it on you as it happened, Raven. I got a bug in my kidney, four years ago in Tokyo. There's this specialist I saw in Paris who told me to go to Marienbad. Giselle and the others were in Czechoslovakia, trying to set up some kind of film deal. We met and got to talking about Spain and Beltrán. I told her that he had a house near me and that I'd met him. You know the way it goes, a good-looking chick, so you make the most of it. She asked me if I could fix an introduction. I put her in touch with Beltrán's secretary and here they are.''

It seemed to hang together yet certain elements baffled me. ''You mean Giselle's the extent of your interest?''

''Was,'' he corrected and winked. ''I'm not the romantic type. If I play guitar and nobody comes to the window I move on. You know?'' He winked again.

''You're going to do your eye an injury,'' I pointed out. I sensed what was coming. I wasn't the only one in whom old habits died hard. ''I bet you checked them all out.''

''Sure,'' he said, looking at me as innocently as he could. ''I like to get my facts straight.''

Wolfie's sources of information would be as good as mine if not better. ''And what did you learn?''

He removed the cheroot from his mouth. ''Giselle's stepfather teaches law at Stanford. Abbott was a news cameraman with CBS.''

''And Christian?''

He allowed himself a quick secret smile. ''A degree in the liberal arts and a square mile of dirt that produces a thousand barrels of medium-grade oil every day. Three hundred sixty-five days a year. No living relatives.''

I felt as if he were pushing me back from the net, getting himself set for one booming volley.

"Why? You don't need money and you're fifty-four years of age. You wouldn't survive a stretch in the slammer.''

"I'm not *going* into any slammer,'' he remarked with assurance. "This guy is a shoo-in, given time to find the right bait.''

"You don't *have* any time,'' I argued. "With your record you can't afford it. One wrong move and a jailer's going to be peering up your arse for the next ten years. And that's another thing. Whatever these people are up to, you're part of it. You visit their house. You're seen with them. You introduced them to Beltrán.'' His smile irritated me. I was trying to protect him.

He opened the door and fanned air into the car, looking down at his white buckskin shoes. "I still say you're wrong. There has to be another reason for her using two names.''

"There is,'' I said. "That's why these people are nervous at the thought that I might have seen both documents.''

It was odd, looking at him and not knowing whether he was on the level or not. He had money and the record said that he was straight. My hunch was that he was too fat a cat to jeopardize his liberty. Yet if he *was* involved, I wanted to know how deeply. Put it down to curiosity. If you chase a man long enough you acquire a sort of proprietorial interest in him. I told him about my drive out to the villa, the scene by the pool, my sojourn hidden in the house.

He massaged the top of his head, looking like a man who's recently found that his pocket has been picked. "I just can't believe it,'' he said at last.

"Then you'd better start,'' I retorted. "You're a four-time loser, buster. You've got three convictions for felony. The next one sends you to the head of the class."

He blinked. "Twenty-five years ago and none in Europe."

"Never mind how long ago or where," I answered. "You are *it*."

He looked out across the tarmac. The windsock lifted in the breeze. Immaculately dressed children were doing their best to ruin one another's eyesight in the sandpit. Their parents watched them indulgenty. He took a deep breath.

"I've seen shots of their work. They did a program on David Hinckney — Hockney, is it? And another on this painter Eugene Deckers in Paris. Names people know."

"The passport," I repeated.

He fumbled for a match to relight his smoke. "Okay, the passport. So they destroy it. Then what have you got, nothing."

I'd already been there, thinking it out while pacing the grass. "They're not like us, Wolfie. They're crackpot amateurs. You can't apply the normal rules."

"Very good," he replied. "Now let me ask you something else. Who's going to rip off something he can't either use or sell?"

"Nobody," I admitted. "Not unless he was going to treat it as some kind of a quid pro quo."

"A *what?*" he demanded.

He's done the same kind of thing to me all too often. I lifted an eyebrow at him. "If you'd been exposed to a classical education . . ."

"Yeh, well," he said. "I was exposed to the Sarnia Reformatory. You'll have to talk down to me."

"A bargaining counter," I elaborated. "You give me this and I'll give you that."

He looked at me pityingly. "You're losing your marbles, Raven. This Indian's got more money than Beltrán."

He was making a better show than I was and we both knew it. "So use your imagination," I said. "Rack your

57

brains and think what kind of score these people could be dreaming up. You can give me the answer over dinner. What's more, I'll buy the meal. I owe you that for the pleasure you bring into my life.''

He unfastened the door and shoved his head back through the open window.

''You're carrying on like some bullshit sleuth and all because a gal uses two names. It's giving me bad vibes, Raven.''

''There's something about this that isn't kosher,'' I said obstinately.

He turned the corners of his mouth down. ''So detect. You're supposed to be the detective.''

''I've got a hunch it's something to do with Beltrán's paintings,'' I said.

We stared at one another, the idea locking our gazes. ''I don't think you know a lot about thieves in spite of everything,'' he said. ''You just don't steal what you can't use.''

''Amazing,'' I said. ''Never mind, tomorrow will tell. You'll have no problem. With your legs you can always be part of the floor show.''

He put his finger in his mouth and bit off an imaginary knuckle. ''I suppose you mean well,'' he said, giving me one of his grins.

''Hardly ever,'' I answered. I watched as he backed out and tore across the parking lot. By the time I reached the crossroads, the thundercloud gray Volkswagen was out of sight. I was glad that the air had cleared between us but it was obvious that the talk had left Wolfie badly shaken. He can't take shocks that are not of his making. When he's sure, he likes to be certain. The Volkswagen was parked by the tennis courts. A foursome was still playing. I left the Seat alongside the convertible, climbed the steps to the pool and threaded my way through the oiled, prostrate bodies. The two Danish girls were swimming topless, the waiters watching them from behind the restaurant curtains.

I walked through to the bar to find Wolfie sitting at a table with the Colombian sisters.

"Over here!" he called, beckoning vigorously.

I ordered a beer and carried the glass across. Though I knew the sisters by sight, I'd never been formally presented. Wolfie made the introduction hurriedly as if he thought I'd escape.

"This is a good friend of mine, John Raven. Señora Alatren and Señora Weber."

Their fingers were slivers of crimson-tipped ivory weighted with expensive jewelry. Smooth, lustrous hair, parted in the center, wrapped their catlike faces.

"Maria-Teresa," smiled the younger.

"Helena."

The invitations to first-name familiarity were made with displays of flawless teeth. Both women were wearing silk knit trousers, gaucho-type shirts and belts with solid-gold buckles. I'd seen the car they drove, a convertible Rolls with C. D. plates. I put their ages at between thirty and forty. Each had the offhand, slightly masculine manner of the sophisticated Spanish woman. The sisters were drinking stingers. Wolfie was on his champagne and juice mixture.

"We were talking about Beltrán's party," he said. "The girls know him from Madrid and New York."

I nodded politely. "He sounds quite a character."

The mole on the side of Maria-Teresa's nose was artificial but the effect on the creamy skin was startling.

"Pablo can be a bore but his parties are always good value."

Her sister's voice was a careless contralto that left words dangling in the air. Both of them spoke accentless English.

"I wouldn't say always. Personally, I find these transvestite affairs very tiresome. But the men seem to enjoy it for some reason or other. More than the women, I think."

Wolfie drew in his gut. "It's the times, Helena. Good men are thin on the ground."

Maria-Teresa's smile was deadly. "And when you find them they're always too sure of themselves."

Helena leaned forward behind her cigarette and lit it for her. She blew a steam of smoke at her sister.

"You are always so unpleasant to poor Wolfie. I don't know why he bothers to talk to you."

Wolfie winked but his heart wasn't in it. "I'm crazy about her and she knows it."

Waiters had lit the candles in the restaurant and people were going in. Helena looked at her watch. "I'm afraid we have to leave. We've having drinks with some people."

Wolfie and I came to our feet. I bent my head over the diamond-heavy fingers. Maria-Teresa's topaz eyes held mine for a second.

"Perhaps we shall see more of one another? You are going to the party, of course?"

"I don't know," I said.

"We hope so," Wolfie said quickly. "Though I understand that the guest list has already been sent to the police."

"The *police?*" echoed Maria-Teresa. "What do they have to do with it?"

"*The Dirección General de Seguridad,*" said Wolfie. "Your boy friend's going to be there, remember. His Excellency Don Jesus-Maria Alatren y Peralta."

Her face cleared but she sounded unconvinced. "It really is too ridiculous. I mean Jesus-Maria and Pablo with police guards."

Wolfie spread his hands. "He's a minister. Enjoy your meal."

We waited till they'd reached the bar and then walked into the restaurant. A dozen or so people were seated including the Graebners. The maître d'hôtel bustled over and showed us to a window table, snapping his fingers for the scurrying waiters. Candles glowed on starched linen, softening the lines on Wolfie's face. His head came forward on his neck.

"I've got the feeling that Maria-Teresa fancies you. Do you get that impression or not?"

"Not really," I said. I sprinkled some salt on my bread. "But then I don't have the same high opinion of myself that you seem to have. Not in these matters, anyway."

The Danes were sitting by the edge of the pool, drinking. The two girls were still topless, their tanned boyish breasts glistening in the last of the sun. Wolfie dragged his eyes away reluctantly.

"I don't like this business, Raven. You've got me worried."

The bread had cleansed my palate and the red wine was full-bodied. "You haven't come up with any ideas?"

"Ideas!" he exploded, as if I'd insulted him. "What do you want from me, for Crissakes?"

"Keep your voice down," I counseled. "Unless you want everyone else in the room to hear. What I want from you is a little low cunning. God knows you had enough of it in the past. You're not conning these people, Wolfie. They're conning *you!* This may sound illogical — even immoral — but it happens to be true."

The clear soup tasted of sherry. He pushed his plate aside. "Then why don't you go to the law? Okay. So you tell them who you are, an ex-detective from Scotland Yard. There's a foreigner here, working with the approval of the authorities. And you happen to know that she's traveling on a forged passport."

I wiped the soup from my mouth. The sun was going down toward the Portuguese border.

"You're not being consistent, Wolfie. We're not even sure who is real, Dale or Degenhardt. Suppose I go to the police. We can be certain of one thing: if it's false, the passport's going to be well and truly out of sight by then. I can just see my reception, the outraged look on everyone's face. Beltrán's would be livid. With the kind of whack he has I'll be standing at the frontier with my bags packed in fifteen minutes flat."

The roast duck was doing nothing for his digestion. He poked at it halfheartedly and buried his nose in his wine glass.

"In other words you're not going to the law?"

I shook my head. "No."

"So what are you trying to do?"

I leaned forward, both elbows on the table. "Look, I *know* these people are up to some kind of villainy, so two things: One. I want the satisfaction of being able to say 'I told you so.' Two. I'm trying to keep you out of jail. I don't give a fuck about Beltrán, the police or the ethics involved. Have I made myself clear?"

"Crystal," he said. "I keep telling you. You're a disturbed man, Raven. No wonder they wanted to get rid of you. You come on like Sherlock Holmes. All you need is a God damn fiddle."

"Sleep on it," I advised. "And, above all, don't panic. We'll think of something between us. By the way, the duck was superb. Just the thing to serve on the houseboat on foggy evenings. I'll have to ask the chef for the recipe."

His eyes and mouth were sour. "You're in the wrong business. You're a comedian. I can't imagine what life's going to be like without you."

I called for the bill and signed my name across it. "It'll be difficult but not impossible."

"Why couldn't you have stayed in England?" he asked plaintively.

I eased the sting on my buttock. "And sent you food packages in jail? Make no mistake, Wolfie, you're *involved*. You've been involved from the moment you made a play for Giselle. You pay for the brandy."

It was served with due ceremony. Balloon-shaped glasses were warmed over a methylated spirit flame, then the wine waiter's white-gloved fingers decanted the amber-colored Carlos 3. I looked through the large picture window. It was after ten. Moonlight etched the cedars black against a dark purple sky. Occasional headlamps swept through the trees but apart from this there was no sign of life. Night joined sky,

sea and land together till it was difficult to tell where one
ended and the other began.

A waiter's voice interrupted my reverie. "Señor Raven?"

I looked up. "Yes?"

"*Telefono, Señor.*"

"Who is it?"

He shrugged. "*Una señora, Señor.*"

The phone was installed in a seventeenth-century sedan
chair that Wolfie had found in Burgos. I shut the door and
picked up the receiver.

"John Raven."

I think I must have known whose voice would answer but
the sound sent the adrenalin racing again.

"This is Giselle Dale. Have you finished dinner?"

"Just," I said.

"I was wondering if you'd like to come out here and have a
drink?"

I settled my weight against the padded upholstery. "You
mean now?"

"I mean now. I'm alone. The others are out and they won't
be back until late."

The Colombian sisters were making their way to their
table, Helena conducting an unheard orchestra with stylized
movements of her hands and arms. Wolfie had his back to
them, morosely working on his second brandy.

Giselle's laugh had a tinkle of mockery. "You don't sound
exactly wild with enthusiasm."

I hesitated, imagining her face, the derision in her eyes. I
could hear the Nilsson tape playing in the background. There
was no finesse about her performance. She was exposing her
hand deliberately, bent on a confrontation.

"I'd like it," I said slowly. "I'd like that very much."

She laughed again but this time as if she was genuinely
pleased. "Then I'll see you in a few minutes."

"There is just one thing," I said. Whatever she guessed or
suspected, there was no way she should know of my visit the
night before. "I don't know where you live."

She made a small sound of amused apology. "Of course not. How stupid of me. Look, you take the coastal road and drive west. It's about five miles out of the village. You'll see the house posted on your left. It's called Villa Florida. Drive up the track and you'll see a gate. I'll leave the light on for you."

I replaced the receiver, her voice echoing in my ears. I walked back to the table. There was ash all over Wolfie's shirtfront and he was well on the way to being bombed. He looked up inquiringly.

"I've just been asked over for a drink by the lady in question."

"And you're going?"

I picked up my lighter and put it in my pocket. "I'm going, yes."

The brandy had definitely affected him. For a moment I thought he was going to take a swing at me but he brushed his hand across his mouth.

"Well," he said grudgingly. "I guess you know what you're doing."

I lifted my shoulders. "I'm not so sure that I do."

He cocked his pale blue eyes at me. "Did she say who else was going to be there? I mean are there other people?"

It wasn't what he meant and I knew it. But I'd no intention of telling him what she had said.

"I don't know," I lied. "All she said was come on over for a drink. What do you think?"

"What do *I* think?" he repeated. "She's going to make a monkey out of you, that's what I think."

"I doubt it," I said. Maria-Teresa was looking across and smiling. I smiled back. "She may well try."

He rolled a cheroot on the table cloth, loosening the tobacco inside, then he lit it, his eyes moody.

"You don't know this broad. You'll tell her your life story before you leave that house."

"That's a chance I have to take." There was a little brandy left in my glass and I finished it. "It just might work the other way around. Why don't you make an early night of it for once?''

He aimed smoke at the space between us. ''Shall I tell you what I'm going to do? I'm going to sit in that God damn bar and wait until you get back is what.''

''Suit yourself,'' I told him. ''But I'd try to take it easy if I were you.''

5

It was warm outside, the night air perfumed with the scent of tuberoses. I took the short cut round the back of the stables, my feet sinking into the bridle path that threaded the pines. The bungalow was stark and still in the moonlight. I was almost at the door when I had the same sensation of being watched. I retraced my steps to the terrace, the rubber-soled shoes making no sound on the tiles. I could see nothing. I unlocked the front door and stood back. Dead air wafted out, still smelling of flyspray. The motor in the drinks dispenser whirred.

My suspicions were lulled by the familiar pattern of sound. I went in and checked the windows before drawing the curtains. Everything looked normal. The light over the bathroom mirror made a yellow skull of my head. The lines from nose to mouth were deeply etched. I brushed my teeth and sloshed a little Signor Ricci on my chest. Memory stirred a dead voice as I did it. *Dear goat — and old one at that!* I brushed my hair, doing my best to get Cathy's voice out of my head. It was myself I was betraying not her. I was hunting for pleasure instead of the kill. I switched off the light and was glad of the darkness. I was getting too bloody morbid, too introspective. Tomorrow would be the same and the day after that and then another and another. The trick was to make the days worth living.

I drove out on the coastal road, thinking about Giselle and Wolfie. He's been hiding behind face after face all his life but just for a second his guard had dropped. The look he had given me across the dinner table had been one of pure hatred. I've never been particularly jealous but I've seen the emotion at work, pushing men to the point of self-destruction. The Diamond Bourse robbery, for instance. I'd worked on it with a couple of cops called Farley and Sands, twenty-six years old and by no means as instructed as I thought I was. A million and a quarter pounds in gem stones had vanished without trace between two points a quarter-mile away from one another. We had two suspects walking the streets without a single piece of evidence against them and a third in Savile Row Police Station on a holding charge. Dave Lyons was a real pro who substituted brains for butchery but he was sixty years old and his wife was twenty-eight. All he had to do was sit tight and hold his tongue and that was that. We could hold him for forty-eight hours and that was all and he knew it. I watched Farley go to work on him, the bluff cop who knows when he's licked but who has to have his say. *Look, Dave. It's only a matter of hours before you hit the street but while you're sitting in a cell Betty's having it off with Mickey Flynn. And that's the kind of guy you work with?* The trouble was the allegation was true. A day later, Lyons put the contents of two twenty-bore cartridges into Flynn's belly. Flynn lasted just long enough to blow the whistle before he died. Remembering this made me worry about Wolfie.

I turned the car onto the lane leading out to the headland. The lantern was lit above the gate. A cricket in the trees grated like a rusty doorhinge. I continued on to the house. There was no sign of the green station wagon. I switched off the motor and sat there listening to the noise of the ocean below. The smell was salty and yet sweet, the sea combining with the flowers. The lower half of the house was in darkness but there were lights upstairs. I went up the steps. The front door had been left open. I could hear the cassette player going in the obscurity. It was still Nilsson. *Takealimeanacoconut andrinkitalldown!*

"Anyone there?" I yelled. My voice echoed in the hallway. The cameras and film were still there and a lot of sound equipment.

Giselle answered from upstairs. "I'll be right down."

A light switch clicked and she appeared at the head of the stairs, holding her dense black hair to one side and smiling at me.

"The door was open," I said. I'd no idea why my voice was defensive.

"I know," she said. She descended the stairs, closed the door quietly and stood with her back against it, her eyes on mine. She was wearing soft washed-out jeans that clung to her thighs and a man's shirt chopped off at the elbows. "I'm glad you came," she added softly.

My whole body was tense with expectancy. The distance between us seemed to crackle with static. She removed her hand from her throat and led the way into the sitting room. A match flared over a fat pink candle. The French windows were open. Moonlight silvered the frieze of bushes at the point of the headland. Glass tinkled as she moved in the shadowed room.

"Scotch?"

"Please," I said. "Water, no ice."

She lit more candles on the mantel. The balloon was still bobbing in the fireplace, its lipsticked mouth grinning. She gave me the glass, her fingers uncurling slowly as she relinquished it. The very way she did it was provocative. She had on the same scent. She fixed herself a Campari-and-soda and I raised my drink.

"To the cheese that tempts the mouse."

She put her head back and laughed, the pulse beating strongly in her throat. "Where on earth did you dig that up?"

"My father had an unlimited supply of them," I said.

"I like it." She moved from behind the drinks table. "Shall we go outside?"

Two chairs on the terrace were angled to face the ocean. There was a package of cigarette papers on the table between them, next to that a silver snuffbox. I lowered myself into the cushions, looking out across the moonlit water. The thought came spontaneously.

"Not a single thing between us and Brazil but that water."

She kicked off her sandals and tucked her long slender feet up under her. "I do believe that you're a romantic."

The noise of the crickets was louder, signaling to one another in the darkness. I balanced my glass on my knee, the breeze on my face, heart beating faster as she moved like a leopard, slowly and certainly. She peeled a couple of cigarette papers from the pack and stuck them together. Then she opened the snuffbox and rolled a fat cylinder of hash. She lit it, inhaled and passed the joint to me. I hesitated long enough for her eyes to register surprise.

"You mean you don't smoke — you're straight?"

"I'm drinking and I'm driving," I reasoned. It irritated me that she could put me on the defensive merely by using her eyelashes.

She leaned across and held the joint close to my lips. "Come on now, you only just arrived. Don't be a spoilsport. In any case you can always sleep here. There's plenty of room."

I found myself counting the beds in my mind. The chair creaked as she leaned even nearer. The acrid smoke tickled my nostrils. After a while I put my glass down and took the joint from her fingers. I cupped it in my hands and inhaled three times, dragging the smoke deep into my lungs before letting it go.

"You'll see," she promised soothingly. She slid from her chair on ball bearings and squatted like a collie by my side. She pushed the sweep of hair from her face and looked up at me. The penciled lines at the corners of her eyes gave her the wide stare of a Siamese cat. "Do you know why I asked you to come here?"

"I'm not sure," I said truthfully.

"But you came, just the same." She smiled, used the joint and passed it back to me.

My mouth was already beginning to parch but I took a couple more drags. Whatever the stuff does to my senses it had never affected my judgment.

"That's right," I agreed. "I came."

She laid one finger very gently on the back of my hand. The effect was like putting a thousand volts into my body.

"A woman knows when someone is interested in her," she said. "When someone wants to take her to bed. Isn't it the same for a man?"

The music was very clear, Nilsson's voice like a bell. Her fingers intertwined with mine and her eyes seemed to be inside my head reading my thoughts. "Relax," she said. "It's Lebanese Gold. Jerry copped it from someone in Madrid."

I heard her with the ears of a stranger, someone who was standing yards away looking up at a silver ship that sailed across the night. The noise of the cricket's wings no longer grated, the sound round, full and mellow.

"It's the same for a man," I said remotely.

She was still squatting on her haunches, her mouth a red flower, her neck its slender, lemon-colored stem.

"I'm not a whore," she said dreamily. "If that's what you're thinking."

My voice belonged to the stranger, too, indulgent and tinged with self-mockery. "I'm thinking about me. John Raven, thirty-eight years old . . ." It was incomplete but I didn't know what came next. Something important.

She moved her head gently from side to side, still clinging to my hand. "John Raven, sad and romantic but chemically right for me. Is that okay with you?"

"It's okay with me," I answered. The rules were flexible. I just hoped that I'd understand them.

The last inch of the joint was smoldering unheeded on the ground. She slapped the last sparks from it with her sandal. I followed her into the house as though in a dream. She stood in the light of the candles, her head bent and her hands joined together. I walked forward, lifted her chin and kissed her on the mouth. Her tongue snaked quickly between my lips. Then she pulled away, her eyes questioning in the flickering light.

"Do you really want me?"

I moved my head in assent, drugged by the sound of her voice. Nothing I knew could have torn me from her then. Neither honor, duty nor loyalty to old memories.

"I want you, yes."

"You're sure of it?" she insisted.

"Sure," I said unsteadily.

She waited ten long seconds then gave me her hand. Her lips parted on her gap-toothed smile.

"Then why are we wasting time?"

I followed her bare brown feet up the stairs. A Navaho woven rug covered the low wide bed. The room was untidy. Lingerie was strewn across the sofa. Bottles of make-up cluttered the windowsill. She closed the bathroom door behind her. I heard water running. I pulled off my clothes and slipped between the sheets. The bathroom door opened and the lamps were extinguished. My eyes gradually adjusted to the darkness. She was standing naked in the doorway with the moonlight behind her. I could see her face, still smiling. I heard the slither of her feet and threw the sheet back. Suddenly she was in bed on top of me, her weight forcing my head deep into the pillow. The musky female smell of her body was strong. She lowered her mouth close to my ear.

"Isn't this what you came for—this and this and *this*?" Her fingers touched my body intimately, forcing response and I entered her. She rode me savagely, pinning my shoulders down, timing herself to our accelerating rhythm. Her back arched and she gasped, locking her body to mine in the last blinding ecstacy. Her nails raked my back and I drifted off into gentle rain and darkness.

I must have dozed. I can remember waking and looking around the unfamiliar outline of the room. There was an illuminated travel clock on the dressing table. It was earlier than I thought, just before midnight. Giselle was breathing deeply beside me, eyes closed, her hair a dark fan on the pillow. I lifted myself up on my elbows. I had to find water. My mouth tasted of tarnished silver. I was just about halfway out of bed when a brilliant flash lit the room. My brain snapshoted the tall figure standing in the doorway. It was Abbott. I felt the top sheet being dragged back, the softness of Giselle's breasts pressing against my shoulders, her hand between my legs. More flash bulbs popped in rapid succession as Abbott moved around the bed, angling his camera at us. Then the lights came on. Abbott was leaning against the windowsill, holding a Polaroid camera and smiling broadly. There was nothing malicious about his smile, he looked as if he was genuinely amused. He stood there, relaxed, as Giselle grabbed a towel from the floor and wrapped it around her waist. She picked a Sullivan Powell from the pack on the bedside table.

"Where's Lance?" she demanded.

Abbott kicked an exploded flash bulb against the wall. "Changing his God damn pants. He tore the others getting in the bungalow window."

The conversation continued, neither of them even glancing at me. I pulled up the sheet, defenseless and outraged. "What the hell *is* all this?" I asked shakily.

Abbot swung the gold fish on the chain around his neck. "I got a couple of frontals," he said interestedly. "Cute."

Giselle blew out the match. She stood by the bed, letting the smoke dribble from her mouth. "Watch this bastard, Jerry. He's tricky."

Abbott's smile grew broader. His right hand lifted from the windowsill, holding a snub-nosed police special. It was pointing straight at my stomach.

"You've no *idea* how tricky! Wait until you hear his telephone conversation with Scotland Yard."

Her eyes widened, her mouth contemptuous. "You make me sick," she said to me, her voice very deliberate. She switched away and slammed the bathroom door after her.

Abbott ruffled his blond curls, his face sympathetic. "*Women*," he said confidentially. The gun was steady, his expression curious. "What *is* your angle, Raven. I mean you're not a cop any longer; who are you working for?"

"No one," I said. My mind was empty. All I knew was that I was in danger. The hands of the travel clock had moved past midnight. The bathroom door opened. Giselle came out dressed in the jeans and man's shirt, her scrubbed face shining with water. She'd tied her hair back with a black velvet ribbon. She crossed the room, picked up the Polaroid camera, looked at the prints it had ejected and dabbed scent behind her ears. I stared at her dumbly, wondering what came next. She put her toe under my trousers and punted them at the bed.

"For Crissakes get yourself out of there and stop looking as if you'd been raped!"

She sat on a chair, playing with the ribbon at her neck as I pulled on my pants. "You liked?" she asked suddenly, putting her head on one side.

She was worse than an animal, I thought, with her cynical smile. I had no excuses. But the idea of having shared something with her repelled me. She had been in my blood but the magic was blown. I pushed my feet into my shoes and buttoned up my shirt.

"On the thin side, isn't he?" asked Abbott.

"Thin but romantic," she said.

My brain darted past the menace of the gun, down the stairs and out into friendly darkness. I fished a bent cigarette from my pocket and lit it.

"You're going about this the wrong way," I said quietly.

Abbott's face filled with mock admiration. "Hear that?

We're going about this the wrong way. This guy's not to be believed!"

Giselle waved him down impatiently. "How much of your business do you usually tell your friends, Raven?"

"I don't know what you mean," I said. "What friends? How much of what?" I shifted my weight cautiously. The window behind Abbott was open.

She took the gun from Abbott as if reading my mind. "You know what I mean. How many people have you told about that passport?"

I looked from the gun into her dark hostile eyes. "Passport?"

"He's a doll," Abbott said lightly and walked to the top of the stairs. "Bring the tapes up, Lancy," he yelled. He came back, fluttering his eyelids at me.

I couldn't take my gaze from her face, stunned by the open contempt that I saw there. She was completely sure of herself, of the sensuality that would captivate wherever and whenever she cared to use it. For the first time in my life I knew that there were such women. Footsteps tiptapped up the stairs. Christian appeared carrying a tape recorder. He'd cleared a space for the tape deck, looked across at me and winked.

"We're going to whack you out," he promised.

"Just play the tape," Giselle said patiently.

The spool started to turn. I smoked my cigarette, remembering the sensation of being watched, my presentiments of danger. I should have known. Abbott was a trained sound-cameraman. It must have been child's play for people like this to plant a bug in the bungalow. Then they'd dragged me out here so that they could retrieve it. That and take their pictures. I was a great example for a man who'd done his stint on the Vice Squad. I listed with my head down as the recording of my conversation with Soo unwound. The device they had used was sensitive. Not a word or inflection was missing. Christian finally thumbed the stop button. We sat there in a silence broken only by the wash of the sea and the sounds of the crickets.

"Jesus *Christ!*" Giselle said with feeling.

Abbott yawned delicately. "I told you it was bad."

"It's worse," said the Indian. "And all because Madame has to leave her fucking passport in the car." He straddled his chair, his dark brooding face considering me.

Abbott was whistling softly, his fingers beating out the rhythm on the windowsill.

"You know what I think?" Giselle said suddenly. "I think we go right ahead as planned."

"That we have to do in any case," said Abbott. "The question is what do we do with *him*."

"I've got that one worked out," she said carelessly.

Abbott viewed his nails and smoothed an eyebrow. "You're congratulating yourself again, baby, or hadn't you noticed?"

"She's noticed," Christian said pointedly. "I say whack him out. Take the bastard up in the chopper and drop him in the ocean. He'll never be heard from again."

I thought of the stretched-faced thugs I'd known and their threats, the whispering voices over the phone promising mutilation. In a strange way, these people were far more sinister. Abbott was like a choir boy strangler.

Giselle stroked her throat with her free hand, her eyebrows interrogating me. "Don't let this pair of queens fool you, Raven. They're mean and they're jumpy. You'd do a whole lot better talking to me."

I put my cigarette out. "That's all I want. The chance to talk, to you not to them."

"Alone, of course." Her tongue explored the gap between her teeth. "At this range I can blow your balls off, you realize that?"

I put the ashtray on the bedside table, keeping every movement slow and overt. "I realize it, yes. The story isn't complicated. It won't take long to tell."

Abbott made a sound of digust. "You're not going to go for this shit, are you, Giselle?"

She gestured toward the door. "Leave us alone, Jerry. I

promise you I know what I'm doing."

"Don't you always?" The Indian's voice was waspish. He stepped over the chair, jerking his head at Abbott. "Come on, we're not needed."

Abbott shut the window and looked around the room. Then he shrugged. "Ah well, keep the faith, lovers!" The door closed.

I raised my head cautiously, taking in the details of the room. A scarf trailed from the iron lamp bracket. Wilted tuberoses drooped in an ugly vase. The half-liter bottle of Estée Lauder was open, its cap on the dressing table. Someone had spilled wine—blood—on the sisal mat and dust had collected on the bag on top of the clothes closet. I could read the Lufthansa tag. MUNICH.

She lit another Sullivan Powell, managing her matches without relinquishing the gun. The safety catch was off and she handled the weapon familiarly.

"I called Wolfie after you left the club. He'll expect you when he sees you."

I was still sitting on the bed, the imprint of her head in the pillow beside me. I made a small gesture of defeat. "What kind of a woman are you, anyway?"

"Different," she said. "And definitely not your kind."

I could hear the music going downstairs, Christian's voice, loud and quarrelsome. I looked for the truth in her face.

"Isn't there a single bloody thing that you respect?"

"A number of things," she said in a flat voice. "But let's get back to you. You wanted to talk, remember."

I moistened dry lips. The tarnished-silver taste was still in my mouth. "I never even heard of you until yesterday, until you left that passport in the car. You'll just have to believe that. I'm not even sure now that I know your right name. I had very good and personal reasons for leaving the Police Force. Reasons that left me on nobody's side but my own. You have to know that I don't give a fiddler's fuck about what people call justice. I've come to believe in expediency. Whatever happens to be expedient for John Raven.''

She was watching me from half-closed eyes, the smoke curling up past her right cheekbone.

"I guess you called Scotland Yard from the village, right? And a few hours later you have all the information you need. How is it that an ex-cop is able to do this?"

I lifted a shoulder. "Under the Old Pals Act. By having a friend who's willing to sidestep the rules.''

They were playing the Nilsson tape downstairs, for the twentieth time. The clock showed twenty-five minutes to one. She jiggled a loose sandal on the end of her big toe.

"Why bother calling in the first place? You're not a cop any more and you've just said that the law doesn't mean anything to you.''

I was out on the lake where the ice was thinnest and one false step would sink me. "It's difficult even for me to appreciate this. I mean it's hard to explain.''

"Try me,'' she invited, still swinging her sandal.

"Okay,'' I said. I hoped it came out better than it sounded in my head. "There *was* only one reason at first. I wanted you physically. I was ready to use anything that Soo could dig up if it would have helped me get you.''

"Fascinating,'' she said. "Do tell.''

I could see myself in the wall mirror, a tousled figure-of-fun. About as impressive as a molting crane.

"Soo is one hundred and one percent reliable. I knew that whatever he said just had to be right. Okay, so you weren't criminals. It didn't stop me wondering why you'd have a passport and a driver's license in different names. So I started to think of reasons, the innocent ones first.''

Abbott's voice sounded halfway up the stair. "Everything all right in there?''

She put her head on one side, her expression momentarily irritated. "What kind of a question is that?'' she called back. She smiled across the bed at me. "And what did you finally decide?''

"I'm not sure,'' I admitted. "But whatever your reasons

are, you're too intelligent to think that they're worth killing me for. I'm not a real threat to whatever it is you're into. Believe that, Giselle, it's true.''

She slipped her long brown foot back into her sandal. ''Why couldn't you have minded your own business?'' she asked composedly. She was completely cool, without the first hit of sensuality, as though the bed we had lain in together never existed.

''I'm trying to do that now,'' I urged. ''It isn't too late. Just tell me what you want from me.''

Her eyes were like an eagle's, fixed and unwinking, willing me to confession.

''It's the truth,'' I said.

''You're a fool,'' she said finally. ''Even for the fuzz you're a fool.''

The back of my shirt was drenched with sweat but the feeling of danger had lifted. A lifetime ago I'd climbed damp steps in some foggy dockside tenement, a rookie in clumsy boots investigating a routine disturbance complaint. A shadow on the stairs became a hand holding the edge of a straight razor against my jugular. I can still recall the stench of beer and vomit, the man's labored breathing behind me, the woman lying on the floor through the open doorway, the odd feeling that in seconds I'd be dead. The woman's scream had saved me.

Giselle stretched with a cat's control of muscle. ''This friend of yours in London didn't do too well, darling, did he? Maybe I should fill you in a little. Let's start with Lance? Did you ever hear of the Dartry Clinic?''

I shook my head. She waved the gun. ''It's a place where split minds are supposed to be put together very, very expensively. We don't talk about it but Lance was there for a couple of years. Just between you and me, I think it's left its mark. Now Jerry's much less complicated. He likes women when he's too stoned to do anything about it. The rest of the time he likes men. Which leaves me. I can sew and do embroidery, I speak three languages fluently and play a fair bit of Scarlatti from memory. My stepfather lectures in law at Stanford University. How am I doing, are you getting warm?''

I pressed my lips together, trying to make sense of what she was saying. One thing was sure, Her contempt for me was absolute. She seemed to take pleasure in giving me these details about her background. Yet broken down, the information was no more than I could have determined on the end of a couple of cables. They were all unhinged. That had to be the answer. All three of them freaks. And as I'd told Wolfie, you couldn't apply normal rules.

I leaked the denial cautiously. ''I'm sorry. I don't get it, no.''

She tucked the small gun in the breast pocket of her shirt. ''Then you disappoint me. Let's go downstairs.''

She made it plain that I went first. The front door was bolted, the French windows closed. The moon had shifted and hung in a powdering of stars. Abbott was lying on the floor on a goatskin rug, his head on a cushion. Christian scowled from the sofa. Giselle switched off the music.

''Stand over there where we can see you, Raven.''

I followed her finger and stopped in front of the fireplace. The kitchen door was shut as well, I could see. She wriggled herself into a place beside Christian on the sofa.

''Raven fancies me,'' she announced. ''That is to say, he did. I don't think he does anymore. And that's why he called this guy in London. It seems that the Inspector was going to blackmail me into his bed.''

Abbott cradled his face in his arms and started to laugh. His back arched and he heaved and finally stopped, sitting up and wiping his eyes.

''I don't believe it! He's a babe in the woods!''

Christian's voice snaked through the amusement. ''I want a word with you people. Can't you understand that this bastard's bad news?''

Giselle looked at him, shaking her head. She pulled the gun out of her breast pocket and held him briefly close.

"Shush, Lance, baby. You're upsetting yourself for nothing."

"Let him ride," said Abbott. "Don't spoil today's turn-on. We're being Dangerous Dan McGrew."

Christian's look was malevolent. "Everything's a turn-on with you, motherfucker. Including that stupid eye shadow. You come on like a Muscle Beach queen."

She'd pushed the gun down between the cushions. For a moment I thought of going through the French windows the way they'd taught me in basic training, back first, my hands protecting the exposed arteries. The mockery in her face made me think again. She was kneading Christian's neck muscles and he was leaning into the pressure like a cat.

"Stop acting like children," she ordered. "Raven wants to make a deal. At least that's what I think he wants."

Abbott raised his head again. "Do we *need* a deal? I mean what *sort* of a deal?"

"That passport," she said simply.

"Oh, that!" He settled himself on the cushion again and closed his eyes.

"Listen," she said. "Do you want to hear something funny? Raven thinks Lance just might kill him. Did you ever hear anything quite as funny as that?"

"No," said Abbott promptly and reopened one eye, looking up at me. "Is that true?"

I drew a deep breath. I'd seen the elaborate cruelty of my sister's two children. This was on the same order.

" 'Might' is the operative word. I think only one of you is capable of murder but I also think you're too smart for it."

"He wants to help us," Giselle said in explanation.

Abbott came up on both elbows. "That's different. What can he do?"

Giselle put her cheek next to Christian's. The color of their hair and eyes was almost identical. "Tell us, Raven. Tell us what you can do."

All three assumed looks of exaggerated interest. Far off, through the French windows, light buoys flashed their warning signals. The sea rolled and boomed below. I did my best to sound both confident and reasonable.

"I think the point is what I *won't* do. I don't know your business nor do I want to know it. You can take my word for that."

"Here comes Sir Galahad," Abbott said with an air of wonder.

Giselle laid a strand of Christian's glossy hair across her face. "I call that very broadminded. Let me see if I've got it straight. You are actually prepared to give us your word that you won't fuck us up?"

"How could I?" I asked. They were playing a game with me, jumping me through hoops.

She made a mustache of the hair, frowning. "Well, you still might go to the police." She made two ironical syllables out of it — *po*-leess.

Moths were banging against the French windows. The stink of hash still hung in the air. I laughed but the sound wasn't right.

"What would I tell them? That passport's out of the way by now and what about the photographs?"

"He's right, you know, Giselle," Abbott said from the floor. He rolled over on his back, holding the Polaroid prints to the light. "Who*ee!*" he said. "I don't believe they'd take him seriously."

Christian jerked his hair out of Giselle's grasp and grabbed the gun. His mouth was thin and mean as he looked at me. "Never mind 'might.' I've found this fucker out. He's the Lone Star Ranger and I'm going to waste him."

"You'll never get away with it." I said. People just don't talk like this but here I was doing it.

Giselle took the gun from his fingers, looked at her watch and yawned. "Tell him, Jerry. I'm getting sleepy."

Abbott jumped to his feet, tall, bronzed and relaxed. He walked behind the sofa, his hand lingering on the girl's cheek as he passed. He was back from the hallway in seconds, carrying a movie camera. He opened the kitchen door and posed there, facing the French windows and the pool. He tapped the casing of the camera and winked at me.

"It's all in here. Every thrilling moment recorded in wonderful picture and sound. Mata Hari and her switched-on inspector."

He opened the French windows, letting in the sweet cool air. I wiped my forehead, bracing myself for whatever came next. Christian lounged off the sofa.

"I'm going to bed." He smiled at me winningly. "Good night, sweetheart."

Abbott leaned down behind Giselle, his face hard and watchful. "Just one thing before you go, Raven. Don't waste your time looking for your passport. It's packed away in one of your bags with some shirts and socks and an ounce of Lebanese Gold. There's everything there that a switched-on dude like you would need for a funky weekend. Behave yourself and you'll get the bag back. Otherwise it goes to the law. Have we made ourselves clear?"

I swallowed the egg in my throat. My voice sounded like a clarinet.

"You've made yourselves clear."

Giselle dusted the ash from her jeans, smiling as she let me through the front door. I heard her call after me.

"Drive carefully, hear now?" Then the door slammed and the hallway lights went out. I switched on the ignition. Headlamps stabbed the back of the station wagon. My hands were shaking on the steering wheel. I'd been ridiculed and humiliated. I'd been hunted, all the time thinking that I was the hunter, my skills derided. This woman had reversed my judgments and emotions, using them against me and there wasn't a bloody thing I could do about it.

I slammed into bottom gear and put my foot down hard. It was almost two o'clock when I drove through the club gates. Wolfie's lights were still on and people were in the bar. I turned the wheel, sending the small Seat hiccupping down the lane to my bungalow. I could see the broken window from the carport, the curtain sucking in through the damaged pane.

I let myself in through the front door. Thieves are neither tidy nor respectful of other people's property. The bedroom looked as if a cyclone had hit it. Drawers had been emptied onto the floor, the bed overturned. There was broken glass everywhere. One of my bags was missing but I suppose that I still had hope even then. This just *couldn't* be happening to me. I felt in the table drawer. My heart sank like a stone in a well. It had happened all right. My passport was gone.

A mosquito zoomed in the light. I made the bed and started picking up the clothes from the floor. Then I stripped and stood under the shower, scalding my body free of Estée Lauder. I brushed my teeth, collected a beer from the cooler and drank it in the darkness, listening to the drone of the mosquitoes. I'd read somewhere that only the females sting. I suddenly remembered something that Cathy had said all that time ago. *You know what your problem is, dearest goat? You've got a perverse will to lose.* She'd known me a whole lot better than I'd known her but it just wasn't true. People didn't understand. There were times when you had to go against the odds no matter what the consequences, so that it looked like a forlorn venture. But *real* losing, like with these bastards tonight, left me hostile and resentful. Their tactics baffled me. I had no inkling what they were up to and no idea how I was going to even the score between us. I fell asleep trying to put the pieces together.

6

THE ALARM in my head went off at seven-thirty. I opened gummed eyes cautiously like a prisoner waking in a cell for the first time, refusing the memories that had put him there. The orange curtain billowed through the broken window-pane, bright in the morning sunshine. I kicked the sheet back and stretched till small knots of pain formed behind my ears. The bathroom mirror showed scabbed nailmarks that ran the length of my shoulderblades. I dabbed them with antiseptic, brushed my teeth and leaned my forehead against the mirror, dribbling water into the bowl. Scoops of dark-edged flesh supported my bloodshot eyes. I opened my mouth, wincing at the sight of my coated tongue. I looked like some hardened dregs-drinker waiting to crawl into police court, a thousand years old and lost to self-respect.

I opened the curtains and stepped out onto the terrace. A fighter plane trailed vapor high in the cloudless sky. Whatever had happened to me, everything else was unchanged. Ants swarmed in the grass. The fat trees dozed. I could hear the maids singing in one of the neighboring bungalows. I threw myself into my exercises, pitting my will against protesting muscles till sweat rolled off my body. Then I wrapped myself in the toweling robe and sat at the terrace table composing my first letter. I've never been a good correspondent, not even with Cathy. Life went on and feelings changed. It was sometimes better not to record them on paper.

My dear Sister . . . I crossed that out and wrote *Dear Anne: I'm enclosing a check for the children. How about buying them something they want for a change and not what they need?* She wouldn't approve of that but then she rarely approved of what I did. I tapped the Ducados from the pack and put it next to my lighter. A German rocket killed both my parents in 1944. I was eight years old, Anne five years younger. From the moment they took the braces off her teeth, my sister took over the running of our family. As far as she was concerned I'd done nothing right since I'd left Harrow. My choice of career offended her deeply. She reminded me that our great-great-grandfather had founded the firm of timber merchants that provided our income. This was true enough. A cast-iron statute in an Ipswich public garden perpetuated his memory. No Raven had ever been a policeman, she said. The way I lived was absurd, on a damp smelly houseboat, eating my meals standing up, spending my time and money in those horrid discothéques. And as for the women I associated with, the less said the better. I wrote the check and finished the letter. *The place is full but I wouldn't call the guests exactly interesting. Nothing much happens except that I catch up on my reading, swim a little and tend to over-eat. The weather is glorious.*

The maids arrived with breakfast. Alarmed by the broken window, they clucked solicitously, looking at me. I pantomimed a fall in the darkness, grabbing at the curtains till their round shining faces showed understanding. The one with the mustache nodded vigorously and swept up the pieces of glass.

"Que suerte, hombre!"

I lit the Ducados and picked up the phone. Wolfie's voice sounded ill-humored and sleepy.

"What the hell's on *your* mind?"

"I got robbed," I said.

"Huh," he said and then yelled as he got the message. "Did you say *robbed?*" The indignation in his voice was ironical but then there's no one more indignant than the man whose dog craps on his own doorstep.

"I'd better see you," I said. "In a half-hour's time; can you make it?"

"I'll wait here for you," he answered.

I went back onto the terrace. The next two letters took me longer to write. The first was to my lawyer, George Ashley. George has no room in his head for fantasy but he's completely reliable. The second letter was addressed to His Excellency, Her Britanic Majesty's Ambassador to Spain, in Madrid. I sealed all three letters. The only document that had been taken was my passport. My pesatas, traveler's checks and driver's license were still in the table drawer. I found a blue linen shirt and denim pants and stuffed the pockets with my possessions. I shut the front door behind me, suspicious now of everything that I saw and heard. I was taking nobody and nothing for granted. I drove down to the village and sent the letters by registered mail. By the time I got back, the scene at the pool was the usual damp, boozy, boisterous extravaganza that I did my best to avoid. Graebner was floating on a rubber raft, as near as he could to the topless Danish girls. Some American kids from the naval base at Santa Maria were clowning on the high-diving board. The Paris merchant-banker was doing his best to ignore the flirtation between his well-preserved wife and the walnut brown chair attendant. The Colombian sisters were sitting under a parasol playing backgammon, just out of splash range. I made my way across to them.

"May I join you for a moment?"

Maria-Teresa waved an invitation and threw the dice. "Mierda," she said and shut the backgammon board, keeping her hand firmly on it. "It is too early in the day. My brains are scrambled." She was wearing a full skirt with a python-skin belt and matching shoes. A lemon silk scarf covered her hair. The emerald on her forefinger was carved in the shape of an owl with ruby eyes. It was difficult to see how she could bend the joint. She moved a foot fastidiously as a dripping body went by. "I think I've had just about enough of this place," she announced.

I lit her cigarette. Helena put the backgammon board in a beach bag.

"You owe me eighteen thousand. Fifteen from last night and three this morning."

Maria-Teresa ignored the remark. "Would you like a drink, John?"

I shook my head. The sisters seemed to change their jewelry as often as their clothes, two or three times a day. They would have been in grave trouble in a city like London where hawk eyes watched for exactly this kind of extravagant behavior.

"When are you leaving?" I asked.

The younger sister's hand indicated a number of possibilities. "It all depends on Jesus-Maria. We're giving him a lift to Madrid."

It was obvious that I was expected to know who they meant. "You'll have to excuse me," I said, "but exactly who is Jesus-Maria?"

She covered my ignorance graciously. "The Minister. The Minister for Information and Tourism. It may be tomorrow, it may be the next day. Jesus-Maria is a bachelor and he likes to enjoy himself. And you?"

An idea was hardening in my head. "I haven't made up my mind. But I'm like you; Las Ventas has just about had me. I suppose the only thing I'll really regret is missing the Beltrán Happening."

Helena looked up from her hand mirror, frowning. "Aren't you going?"

I assumed an expression of regret. "I'm afraid not. You heard Wolfie yesterday. The guest list has been closed because of the police."

They exchanged quick glances. "But that's ridiculous," said Maria-Teresa. "What's it got to do with *Wolfie?*" Her tone diminished the name like a blowtorch working on an ice cube.

I turned my hands. "Well, for one thing, I don't know Beltrán." Maria-Teresa's jewels flashed as she adjusted the scarf on her head, her fingers lingering on the knot.

"You don't have to know Pablo. Half the people there will be strangers in any case. I'll call him after lunch and tell him. Then you can come with us."

My scheme seemed to be snowballing. "You're sure that'll be all right?"

The both looked at me curiously. "Why not?" demanded Helena.

"I don't know," I said. "It's just that . . . look, would it be all right with you if we keep it a secret from Wolfie?"

"A secret from *Wolfie?*" Maria-Teresa's contempt was cutting. She tucked a raven-wing of hair under the scarf. "I wish we could stop talking about this individual. I can't stand the sight of him in any case."

Helena's gesture allowed his existence. "He can be amusing at times. Then that's settled. You come in our car."

"Fantastic." I said. "It's just that he likes to think of himself as the expatriate who's been accepted by local society. I'll be interested to see his face when he finds me on the scene."

Neither of them seemed particularly interested by the prospect. Maria-Teresa lifted her eyes from her fingernails. "Do you know where we live?"

I pointed in the direction of the hard courts. "It's the bungalow in the eucalyptus trees, isn't it? The one with the yellow shutters?"

She showed her small sharp teeth like a cat. "It'll be Spanish hours and nothing will start till late. Call for us about ten and we'll have a drink before we go."

I rose and kissed her hand. "There is one thing. I don't fancy dressing up as a woman."

Her eyes veiled briefly. "I should hope not. Then we'll see you later."

"That's right," I promised. "I'll be looking forward to it."

The way to Wolfie's apartment was past the stuffed fauna in the entrance hall. Domingo was putting flowers on the tables in the empty bar.

I turned left down the wide sunny passage. A couple of spring locks protected Wolfie's door, the top one installed at waist-level, the lower a foot from the ground. I knew the type well. A double turn of the key sank bolts on three sides of the door, securing it against anything but a frontal attack with an ax. I rapped and Wolfie opened the door. He was wearing his usual white chinos and a short-sleeved shirt with an elaborate monogram. His thinning hair was carefully arranged and he'd obviously been reading. The spectacles he'd just removed had left a weal across the bridge of his nose. He kicked the door shut with a moccasined foot, wagging his head as he stepped past me.

"You look terrible!"

The front of the club consisted of two wings separated by the entrance hall. Wolfie's apartment balanced the restaurant. It contained a bedroom, bath and an enormous sitting room. Coarse striped rugs splashed the tiled floor red and yellow. The chairs and sofa were upholstered in black Cordoban leather. An old-fashioned fan revolved in a wire guard on the desk. The only decoration on the wall was a blown up picture of a North Ontario lake under ice. It was a man's room with no concessions made to feminine frippery. I took the armchair facing the window. The putting green outside glistened under the gentle rain from the water sprinklers. Wolfie filled a goblet from the pitcher on the table and handed it to me.

"You'll feel better with this inside you."

It was the usual mixture, champagne and orange juice. He watched me drink it, chasing something along his gum with his tongue.

"What's all this about a broken window?"

I hung one leg over the other. "All in good time. Tell me something. Did Giselle Dale call you last night after I'd left?"

He clipped the edge of the desk with his buttocks, his shirt billowing in the breeze from the fan.

"She did. About ten minutes after you'd left. How did it go?"

I put the empty goblet on the floor beside me. Nothing had ever tasted as good.

"I'll tell you how it went," I said. "Have you ever had a nightmare?"

He blinked at me suspiciously. "Have I ever had a nightmare!"

"That's right. A dream where somebody cuts off your balls or you drop from a height on your head. Death, doom and disaster. That's what I had last night."

I could see through the door leading to the adjoining room. A mirror reflected the cedarwood clothes closet, the cat sleeping on the unmade bed, the framed picture that hung above the pillows of a nude on a rock. Wolfie massaged the weal across his nose. His eyes were pale and direct.

"You'll have to do better than that if you want me to know what you're talking about. So you went there and what happened. Was Giselle alone?"

I refilled the goblet. "She was alone all right. Her playmates were busy taking my bedroom apart. Your pals framed me, Wolfie. It so happened that I had the right sort of larceny in my heart and I was conned. It's as simple as that."

"Well," he drawled, moving to the sofa and snapping his fingers. "It happens to the best of us. Don't say I didn't warn you. I saw this coming."

"Sit down and shut up," I said. "And stop clicking your fingers." I told him what had happened, leaving nothing out. Hearing it all again, sitting in the sun-dappled room with the smell of wet grass in my nose, I realized the extent of my conceit and credulity. It did nothing for my peace of mind.

"I'm going to lock the bastards up," I concluded. "I don't know how but one way or another I'll do it."

He wriggled on the sofa as if his chinos were full of birdshot. "Lock them up for what? You're out of your fucking head. You want my honest opinion?"

"*Honest?*" I said.

The right side of his face twitched as if he'd been stung. "You're an ungrateful bastard, Raven. And there's something else. Stop acting. You're no Laurence Olivier."

I could see the cat through the bedroom door, a rusty-colored monster with battle-scarred ears, wreathing and carrying on against a chair leg. I've had an allergy to cats all my life. Just seeing them makes my eyes water. The hairs inside my nostrils stiffened in anticipation.

"Okay," I invited. "You were going to tell me what I should do."

"Get your arse into Cádiz," he said. "See the British consul. Tell him somebody ripped off your passport and you have to be in England tomorrow. It's a matter of life and death. With your credentials he has no option. Then you take the next plane out. It doesn't matter where. Just out."

I shook my head. "I can't do it. Wolfie. These people have made a right Charley out of me and I just can't walk way from them."

"Okay," he said and replenished his drink. "Let's think. We'll assume that the police aren't going to be interested too much in these pictures. It's the hash you say they've planted in your bag that worries me."

"It worries *you*," I repeated. "Don't you think it worries me?"

He swung away from the desk back to the sofa. "They're busting people left, right and center for drugs. If the law does get hold of that bag, I don't think I'll wait for the movie." He drew his finger across his throat suggestively.

"I'm staying here," I said obstinately. "I'll probably wind up behind bars but I'm not running. I want to know what these people are up to."

He rolled his eyes at me hopelessly. "You don't know what you're saying, Raven. It's delusions of grandeur. You're an ex-cop in a foreign country. You can't go leaning on these kids without falling flat on your face and the passport's destroyed by now. You said so yourself. You don't have a single fucking thing to offer, for Crissakes.''

I poked a Ducados out of the pack and viewed him through a cloud of smoke. "I'm not so sure about that, Wolfie. I might just have what it takes."

He digested the statement carefully before he answered. "What's that supposed to mean?"

The cat was in the room now. "Will you get that animal out of here?" I asked. He took it by the scruff of the neck and deposited it through the window. I waited till he turned. "I have someone working with me."

His surprise was evident. "You mean the law?"

I moved my head from side to side. "A guy I know. Whose side are you on, Wolfie, the kids or mine?"

The pale blue eyes stared back from his honed brown face. "You've got a funny line of conversation. *You* ask me *that?*"

I took a turn as far as the wall and back. "I could be wrong but it's a feeling I have."

His eyes followed me as I paced. "I ought to tell you something, Raven. I'm only here till the end of the month. I sold this place to the Swiss three weeks ago. Four hundred sixty-two thousand dollars. I walk through the door and just keep on going. I don't *have* to care about what some bunch of apple knockers think about me. Understand?"

I wanted to give him the benefit of the doubt but I couldn't. There was something about the way he looked at me, a hostility that even his actor's face couldn't conceal.

"I'm sorry," I said. "Maybe I'm too close to this thing. But I can't get away from the fact that these people went to a lot of trouble with me. A woman on her back. A stolen passport. Hash. They chop me off at the ankles and then turn me loose. It just doesn't make sense."

93

He took his goblet to the desk. "It makes sense to me. They turned you loose because you're no longer a threat."

"How about you?" I asked.

He swung round, pushing his finger against his chest. "*Me?* What have I got to do with it? I've been in that house maybe ten times. I've told you the extent of my interest. How the fuck could I be a threat. I'm not supposed to know what you know anyway."

"I could have told you."

"*You?*" His pale blue eyes were scornful. "An ex-cop!"

"I did tell you," I pointed out.

"They'd never believe it," he said with conviction.

He'd shown me a gun the week before, banging on about what a good shot he'd become. If I asked him to lend it to me, he could hardly refuse if he was on my side.

"I need to borrow your pistol," I said, looking up.

"*What?*" he exclaimed, warding off the suggestion with an outstretched hand. "You see!" he complained to the room at large. "You tell a guy something in confidence and he screws your arse off. Do you mind telling me why, for instance, you need a pistol?"

"I have some unfinished business to take care of," I said steadily.

He took a deep breath. "You know something, Raven. Your breaks are really off. I suppose you realize in your usual all-round wisdom that I don't happen to have a gun permit? That if you go around here blasting off at people, I'm going to be asked a whole lot of questions."

"You're involved to the eyeballs already," I told him. "Everybody's involved and I'm the only one who doesn't know what's going on. Okay, me and possibly you. You have my word that if you give me the gun nothing comes back to the club." I held out my hand.

He looked at it thoughtfully. "What are you up to, Raven?"

I crooked my finger, beckoning. "If you're on my side you'll let me take the gun. Everything's under control. I told you, I've got someone helping me."

He planted splayed legs, rubbing the side of his head. "How do you *mean* — got someone helping you?"

"A friend. Someone who doesn't like what these people are doing to me."

"Great," he said. "That's all we need. A couple of cowboys running around dealing out justice. And you still know nothing."

I wiggled my fingers again. "The gun, Wolfie, or I'll tell them you're a man from the Politburo."

He walked behind the desk and unlocked a drawer. "What kind of crap is that, *Politburo?* I know it's a joke but if anyone hears you I'm in trouble."

He pulled out a Spanish-made .38, loaded the clip from a box of shells and wiped the weapon thoroughly with his handkerchief. He laid the gun on his desk.

"Do me a favor, Raven. Take it into the woods and blow your fucking brains out!"

I slipped the gun inside my shirt and down into my waistband. "Thanks, Wolfie. I'll keep you posted."

He wagged a hand at me. "I never even heard of that gun, remember. Where are you going now."

"Cádiz," I said. "You're better off not knowing about it."

He came to the door with me, his lips forming words that he never spoke. He seemed to change his mind at the last moment and what came out was "We've been around for a long time, Raven. I respect you. Keep away from Villa Florida at least until tomorrow."

An old hand like Wolfie keeps his cool but I could see that he was troubled. "We live in parlous times," I said. "I'll be in touch."

Lunch was being served at the tables by the pool and in the restaurant. I saw the Colombian sisters eating in the bar. I reversed the Seat and aimed it up the driveway. Looking in the rearview mirror I had the impression that I saw Wolfie's curtains move but I couldn't be certain. A hundred yards and

I was out of sight of the clubhouse. I turned right behind the hard courts, past the sisters' bungalow and on to the empty stableyard.

Rhode Island Reds were scratching about among the cobblestones and a blind Labrador lifted its head in the direction of the car. I cut the motor. The small white house behind the eucalyptus trees was where the girl who ran the stables lived. Neither of the two grooms was to be seen. I pulled the automatic out of my pocket, ejected the clip and shucked out the bullets. The business ends were missing. Instead of the usual lead, the brass caps were crimped and harmless. I put the blanks in my pocket and locked the gun in the boot. Most people who used the stables rode either before breakfast or in the cool of the evening. I needed to get to the coastal highway without using my car.

The horse barn was a long lofty building smelling sweetly of hay and carob beans. It was cool inside, insulated by walls two feet thick. A dozen Arabs stamped and dozed in the loose boxes and stalls. Insect repellent mixed with the whitewash kept the flies down to a bearable level. A small owl perched overhead on the rafter, folded in sleepy silence. I walked as far as the tack room, calling without getting an answer. Well-kept saddles and bridles hung on pegs, name plates identifying the animals they belonged to. A picture torn from a copy of *Horse and Hound* was thumbtacked to a green baize board. A girl in a velvet riding cap smiled out at the photographer. The caption read WEST COUNTRY SHOW JUMPER MOVES TO SPAIN.

I walked outside again and climbed the steps to Diana Pole's house. The blind Labrador lumbered after me, swishing its tail gently. Zinnias blazed in the front yard. The door and windows were open. A hinge had turned a horseshoe into a doorknocker. I lifted it and let it fall. The noise echoed in the cool corridor and a girl's voice answered, her Spanish heavily accented.

"*Quién está?*"

The Labrador's blind head nosed toward the sound, the

movement of its tail accelerating.

"It's me," I called. "John Raven — Bungalow Six!"

"Coming," she answered. Heels clattered over the stone flags. According to her own account, Diana Pole was an American veterinarian's daughter to whom London was a once-a-year shopping treat. She was an uncomplicated, leggy girl completely unaware of the high-voltage sexuality she generated. I'd met her maybe half a dozen times and she irritated me. I think it was because she reminded me somehow of Cathy.

She appeared in the passage, wiping fried egg from the corners of her mouth. She had the slim wiry frame of the horsewoman, straight red hair, which she tied with a bow at the back, and the coldest green eyes I had ever seen. She was wearing jeans and Spanish boots with a flowered cotton shirt. Careless, a little grubby and to a certain type of man, I suppose, very much a turn-on. She dropped on her heels by the Labrador and fondled its head.

"What can I do for you?" she asked, looking up at me.

She stressed the last word, almost making it into a challenge. I knew the reason for it. I'd ridden with Wolfie and there was a guarded hostility between her and the Canadian. According to him it went like this. He'd found her through an advertisement and given her a two-year contract to work for him. Once she arrived he saw what he liked and asked her up to the club for drinks and a meal. When the time came for more intimate discussion, Wolfie claimed she had hollered like an outraged duchess. What the hell was it, he demanded indignantly — was he a cripple or something. Two bottles of vintage Bollinger and three hours listening to all that crap about horses. I gathered that she was working out her contract and strictly no more.

"I'd like to go out for half an hour," I said casually.

Her bent head showed a birthmark on her neck. Another thing that reminded me of Cathy. She dislodged a tick from the Labrador's ear with her thumbnail and put her heel on it.

"Riding in *this* heat?" she demanded. She was one of

those competent, bossy kids.

"That's right," I said. "You mean it's forbidden? I'll stick to the shade and we won't be out of a trot."

She came to her feet. "You fell off last time, remember, and I had to spend two hours chasing through the woods looking for a loose horse."

"That was Wolfie's fault," I said. "Charging about all over the place. Come on, now, I'm a lot better than that and you know it." I smiled for whatever use it was.

She sniffed and wiped her nose on the back of her hand. "I've got a sister of seven who rides appreciably better than he does. And you can tell him I said so. You don't propose going out like that, do you?"

Apparently the sandals I was wearing offended her. I glanced down at them and shrugged. "I'll keep my mind on the job," I said humbly. "I need the exercise."

"It's your neck," she said indifferently.

She came out of the barn leading a liver chestnut mare I hadn't ridden before. She leaned against the stone wall, her eye critical as it took me two attempts to get myself into the saddle. I let the stirrup leathers down and tightened the girth. The mare's hindquarters bunched and she bucked hard, shooting me forward. I grabbed at the withers as the girl stepped smartly aside. Her voice was as cool as her eyes.

"You'll break your teeth like that. Try sitting down into the saddle."

I straightened my back self-consciously, hoping that the animal wouldn't bolt till at least we were out of sight. We shot across the stableyard, the mare's hooves striking sparks from the cobblestones. I managed to straighten her out and we cantered up the bridlepath going sideways. I bent low like a jockey, using my weight and sawing at the mare's mouth. Suddenly she was off, the bit and my hair lifted in the rush of air. The bridlepath forked ahead. We swung right in the direction of the south boundary wall. The mare lengthened her stride and the canter stretched into a gallop. I was managing better now, my body balanced, legs gripping hard. Dirt flew up, spattering my face and neck. We covered half a mile in less than two minutes. I reined hard at the wall, dismounted, opened the gate and hauled myself back into the saddle. The mare was blown and ready to trot. The coastal road was just beyond the umbrella pines ahead. The route I had taken was the short side of a triangle, a mile at most. Anyone coming by car from the clubhouse would have to cover five times that distance. A large bird whirred up from a fragrant bush. The smell of the ocean was stronger. I tethered the mare in the dappled shade and walked to the last fringe of trees. The road was thirty yards away, the wired-off bull prairies on my right. I could just see the cutoff to Villa Florida, the headland jutting out above a haze of blue water. I sat down with my back against tree trunk and lit a cigarette. The blank shells had given me the answer to my first question. The next few minutes should answer the second.

I kept my eyes on the bend in the bay toward the village. Sweat was stinging the scratches on my shoulders, reminding me of the woman who'd put them there. It was a sordid memory of something ugly done without passion and I disliked it. Ten minutes went by before the thundercloud gray convertible appeared, coming fast in the middle of the road. I had a clear view of Wolfie at the wheel. He veered left at the signpost and disappeared toward Villa Florida. I remounted and trotted back to the stables.

Diana was sitting on the stone wall, chewing a length of straw. I slipped out of the saddle, pulled the reins over the mare's neck and handed her the loop.

"Very good. Thanks."

"This animal's soaked," she said accusingly.

"Yes, well, she takes a bit of a hold." I flexed one leg after another gingerly. "Or didn't you know?"

The band of freckles tightened across her nose. "You people are impossible."

I massaged my legs where the leathers had rubbed my shinbones. "Thanks. Let the office know how much I owe."

I got out of there as fast as I could without actually running.

My hunch had been right. Whatever Wolfie had to say at Villa Florida was too important to be trusted to the telephone. I had to move quickly. There was no way of knowing how long he would stay with Giselle and company. I drove back to the clubhouse and parked in the same place. It was well after two with the restaurant full and the kitchen fully extended. Nobody noticed me walk around the back of the clubhouse, ducking my head as I passed the arch at the end of the patio. I peered round the end wall. The putting green was deserted, the ball boy eating. I could see a waiter carrying a tray up the steps from the pool. No one else. I put a leg over the windowsill and swung myself into Wolfie's sitting room. The cat stared at me impassively from the sofa. The drawer in the desk was locked but I'd seen Wolfie put the key under the base of the fan. There were two boxes of shells in the drawer, one live, the other blanks. I put my own blanks back and took eight live slugs. I tiptoed to the door, interpreting the noises outside in the corridor. I slid the catch back cautiously. A smell of food filtered through the inch-wide crack. I let myself out and hurried out of the building.

I drove back to the bungalow. The maids had done their work. Someone had repaired the broken pane. I stripped off my soiled jeans and shirt and pulled on a pair of swimtrunks. Then I took the gun and shells out onto the terrace. I loaded the clip, pumped a round into the breech and snapped on the safety catch. I sat there for a while, weighing the gun and remembering. Then I locked the fingers of my left hand on my wrist and sighed on the back wheel of the car. Imagination saw the dusty Seat settle on a bullet-holed tire, then I remembered something else, the indignity of pistol practice. The basement firing range stinking of gun oil and exploded cordite, the Marksman-Instructor's sour Australian accent as my shots thudded home off target.

"Lift, steady and squeeze, Inspector! And let's hope the bugger holds still for you when you meet him!"

I went inside the bungalow and hid the gun under the mattress, then came out again. Nothing much surprised me any more but Wolfie's defection left me perplexed. The answer had to be Giselle but I couldn't help thinking of something he'd said to me the same night he'd shown me the gun. *There are only two things that really matter, Raven. Your liberty and your life and one's no good without the other.*

I shut my eyes, catnapping in the afternoon heat. There were times when some people found that life itself had no further meaning, when the endless succession of days and nights became too much to face alone, till a girl just gave up and filled her stomach with sleeping pills. I found that my eyes were wet and wondered whether it was Cathy I was mourning or just some maudlin regret for the man she thought I should have been, the man who had failed her. The phone bell saved my further self-analysis. It was Wolfie.

"Hi! You're back then. Can I come down for a moment?"

"Absolutely," I said. "I'm on the terrace."

I wondered how he would play it. If he'd discovered the substitution of the shells he'd know I was on to his double-dealing. Which left me with the question of who he was trying to protect. Giselle, almost certainly. He appeared in a couple of minutes, taking the short cut through the woods. I pushed a chair with my foot and he sat down.

"How'd it go?" he asked casually. Too casually, in fact for someone as vulnerable as he was supposed to be.

"It's a good thing to have friends," I answered.

"You've got to find them first," he said, grudgingly. "Where's this one come from?"

"Off a ship," I said vaguely. "A ship that docked in Cádiz." I wanted him to think I had help. If he knew, his friends would know and it just might rattle them.

"Pretty damn convenient," he observed.

I nodded. "Pure coincidence. It happens. Like you being in Marienbad at the same time as Giselle Dale."

He lifted his face, frowning. "What's that supposed to mean?"

"Nothing. Except that there are such things as coincidences."

He wasn't satisfied. I could read it in his eyes. What I'd

said had slipped past his guard.

He swung a leg and hooked his forefinger inside his shoe. "We know one another a long time, Raven, right?"

The approach was always the same, the reminder of something shared. It was as if he was trying to tell me something and ducking out at the last moment.

"A long time," I agreed and waited with the silence stretching.

He cocked his head, affecting a long-range interest in the dog that was foraging in the Graebners' garbage.

"I feel responsible, you know that? If it was a question of money . . ."

The dog was up on its hindlegs, nosing off the cover of the trash can. "I don't fellow you, Wolfie," I said.

He waived a hand. "What I'm trying to say is this. I wouldn't want to see this girl get into trouble over a lousy God damn passport. I like her, sure. I still do."

"Who's talking about a passport?" I asked. "I'm talking about three bastards who deliberately set me up. A woman who made me feel cheaper than I've ever felt before. Why did you give me that gun, Wolfie?"

He was rolling one of his cheroots on the table. He stuck it in his mouth. I reached for a Ducados. There were only three packs left in the carton. I'd smoked seven packs in just over two days. I used my lighter and passed it to him.

"You have found one somewhere else," he said. "If it's mine maybe you won't make a fool of yourself."

He hadn't discovered that I'd been in his drawer. I was sure of it.

"Look," I said. "Do you want to know why I haven't taken your advice — why I'm not in Cádiz at this moment, banging on the consul's door? It's because I'm obstinate, Wolfie. Knock me down and I have to get up. I can't help it — it's like breathing."

He pinched his noise reflectively, looking across at the mended bedroom windows as if he expected to see someone standing there.

"Do you know what we used to call you in the old days, Raven? We used to call you 'Mystery X,' the guy who follows you through a revolving door and comes out ahead. You haven't changed a God damn bit and it just might ruin you."

"And that worries you?" I watched a butterfly zigzag out of the bougainvillea and perch on the windowsill.

He peered round the screen of smoke. "It worries me. I'd feel better about things if I could get just one straight answer out of you."

"Ask away," I invited.

He leaned forward, looking directly into my eyes. "I want to know your real interest. Is it the phony passport or Giselle?"

I took my time, discarding words till I found the right response. "It's retribution, Wolfie. You might call it a touch of the tit for tat."

He held his hand up, making a sound of disgust. "Okay. Okay. Have it your own way but at least do one thing for me . . ."

I nodded. "You already told me. Stay away from Villa Florida until tomorrow. Why's that? I'm not going to blow holes in your girl friend. The gun's strictly for self-protection."

He blew ash from the end of his cheroot. "She's not my girl friend. I couldn't get to first base with her. All I said was that I liked her. Do it, Raven. Tomorrow's another day."

I picked the splinters of cane from between the hairs on my legs. "I hadn't intended going there, certainly not tonight. What would be the use? They'd all be at Beltrán's party, wouldn't they?"

"That's right." His eyes slid away and then he shrugged. "How about your buddy from the boat?"

"He'll do what I tell him," I said.

His face was vaguely reassured. "Well, look: if you want to front these people tomorrow—that includes Giselle—I'll come with you if you like."

"That could be interesting." I took the hand he offered.

"Keep your cool," he said and winked.

I watched him through the trees. I've long since forgotten the fat sergeant's name but he'd summed it all up years ago, the two of us drinking stewed tea in the cafeteria under the Central Criminal Courts. We'd both given evidence in a case that involved a blind pickpocket. I'd had qualms. The sergeant had been avuncular. "Look, son. Don't go wasting no bleeding sympathy on villains like that. They never go straight. They might well make all the right noises but up here" — and he tapped his forehead — "they stay the same. The only thing the buggers change is their underwear."

7

IT WAS almost three o'clock and I hadn't eaten. I dressed and drove down to the village and stopped on the *embarcadero*. Fishermen were sleeping in the shade cast by their boats. High tide had left a rim of seaweed where sand flies hopped and crawled.

I ate in a small dark bar filled with shiny wine casks, making a meal of *tapas:* meatballs spiced with garlic, batter-fried squid tentacles, tiny shreds of sun-cured ham. The wine was the color of a tiger's eye and strong. The bar had emptied by the time I had finished. I left some money on the counter and climbed the hill to the telephone office. Nothing seemed to have altered since my last visit. The same sentry was lounging outside the Civil Guard barracks, the goat had started nibbling a gatepost. I gave the wax-faced operator my lawyer's number in London and took my place in the booth. The fan bearings rumbled with each revolution. It was a matter of time before the whole thing collapsed, bringing the ceiling down with it. The connection was made rapidly. I could hear George Ashley's plumy voice as if he'd just finished lunch and was savoring Havana tobacco and the taste of vintage port.

"John!" he said. "How nice to hear your voice. How are you?"

"Troubled," I said. "And I want you to listen to me very carefully. If your office hasn't had news of me by five o'clock tomorrow night, contact the Yard. Insist on talking to the Interpol Liaison Office. I don't care how you do it but don't let yourself be sidetracked. Have you got that?"

"The Interpol Liaison Office." He was as tolerant as a psychiatrist at the beginning of a tough session. "Yes, I've got all that down, John."

I continued. "And when you're sure you're talking to the right man and *only* then, you tell him you've got grave fears for my safety. Grave fears. And George, there's a letter in the mail that explains everything."

A barge siren sounded in the background. The windows of the house in Kings Bench Walk would be open to the river. His voice was professionally calm.

"Where are you speaking from, John?"

"Spain." Where the rain falls mainly on the plain and suckers like John Raven had their arses nailed to the ground as Wolfie put it. "Don't waste your time with anyone but the man from the Interpol office. It used to be someone called Bailey but that was eight months ago. If you really run into trouble call 01-230-1963 and ask for Inspector Soo. Don't use this number unless you have to. Now, do you think you've got all that, George?"

"I think so, yes." A hint of doubt crept into his voice. "There's one thing I'm not quite sure about. Why am I supposed to fear for your safety?"

I brought the mouthpiece very close. "Because I'm telling you I'm in danger. That's why. Any time after five o'clock tomorrow afternoon you're the senior partner in a highly respected firm of lawyers acting for a client who's in need of police protection. Make it up as you go along but *do* something. The letter explains."

"I doubt it," he said drily. "Unless you've changed your style radically. Can't you give me some sort of clue?"

"No, I can't," I said. "Try *Alice in Wonderland*."

"Does your sister know about this?"

"My sister does *not* know about it nor do I want her to. Just stick to the instructions. Okay?"

"You're sure you're all right, John? I mean, at the present moment?"

"I'm sure about nothing," I answered with feeling. "Except that the deadline is five o'clock tomorrow. Don't make a move before then but once you go, go fast."

I paid for the call and walked down to the parked car. It was almost five by the time I returned to the bungalow. I took the clean laundry off the bed and lay down with my hands behind my head, staring up at he ceiling. Giselle Dale's eyes haunted me. Her smile was contemptuous. Sexuality made her completely sure of herself. She seemed to enjoy it both for its own sake and for the power it gave her to bedazzle her prey. She was a woman without the least sensibility for the feelings of others, an enemy to be hunted down till she cowered in total submission. And when that time came I hoped for the grace to smile just as she did.

I read for a while without making sense of the text. It was already dark when I started to dress. The lights from the neighboring bungalows shone through the pine trees. I put on a green silk suit, an open-necked shirt and Italian shoes that gave me the height of a basketball player. *Exaggerate your defects!* It was a piece of advice that had come from Cathy. She'd known me well and the memories were securely locked into my brain. Reminders of the star we thought would shine forever, of my lack of generosity. *Take my possessions but don't touch my heart*. Cathy again about me.

I looked in the bathroom mirror. The final effect would hardly have pleased my late superiors but then little about me ever had. My coordinator's test of a detective's character had been the length of his hair. Close back and sides being the standard set. The longer the hair, the more suspect its owner. To call a man "trendy" on the sixth floor of New Scotland Yard was equivalent to pulling his file and marking it

"Suggest close observation." I buckled on the bottle green cummerbund and tucked the gun away behind it. If I missed emasculating myself that would already be something. I posed in front of the mirror again, opening and closing my jacket. It was better worn loose, this way the bulge was lost in the folds of the cummerbund.

I walked through the trees to the Colombians' bungalow. The dark blue Rolls convertible was drawn up in front of the open door. The discreet diplomatic plates probably meant that one of their husbands had been in the Colombian Foreign Service. The bungalow was three times the size of mine and every lamp in the place seemed to be burning. I called from the hall but the sound of music drowned my voice. I walked into the sitting room. It was obvious that these women were used to being followed around by maids. The room was in a mess, magazines strewn over the floor, empty coffee cups on the windowsill, dead roses drooping next to a bouquet fresh from the florist. Someone had left a bottle of Balenciaga on top of the record player. There was a card on the mantel that must have come with the flowers. The name meant nothing to me. I turned to find Maria-Teresa standing in the doorway. She was wearing a long flowered dress with ruffles at the throat and wrists. Her beetle black hair was parted in the middle and plaited in the style of an Andes Indian. Hooped earrings dangled down to her shoulders and her diamond watch was shaped like a star. I must have stood there looking at her for fully a minute before I pulled myself together.

"I'm sorry," I said. "It's a long time since I saw anything quite so beautiful." The strange thing was that I meant it. Everything about her had an elegance that was exquisite.

She swept me a low curtsey. "*Gracias, Señor!*" She raised her eyes, the earrings swinging. "Beltrán will be delighted to see you. I won't be a couple of minutes. Pour yourself some wine."

I'd be the first to acknowledge that I was out of my depth. These women were as far removed from me as a giraffe's tail from its mouth. But I needed them to get into that party.

There were two bottles of Wolfie's vintage champagne in an ice bucket. I pulled one out, unraveled the wire and thumbed the cork at the ceiling. The report brought Helena into the room holding her fingers in her ears. She was wearing the same sort of dress as her sister but with a different floral pattern. Her hair was up, displaying a beautifully molded neck set in emeralds. She took me by the hand and turned me round.

"*Hombre! Muy elegante!*"

It's a pleasant thing to hear, no matter how much you tell yourself it doesn't matter, especially from a good-looking woman.

"Thank you," I said, filled a glass and gave it to her.

She sipped the wine and made a face. "Why is it that champagne in Europe must always be so . . . so sour?"

"Dry?" I suggested. "I think perhaps the English are responsible."

Maria-Teresa floated in, used the bottle of Balenciaga on her wrists and behind her ears and took her glass. Her fingers were cool on mine.

"John is used to asking questions, not answering them."

Helena turned her head aside, half-closed her eyes and fired a machine-gun burst of Spanish at the room in general. She lifted her lids at us lazily.

"Beware for your scalp. My sister is a great collector."

I made what I hoped was the right kind of noise. She rounded her mouth.

"Let me guess. She will tell you that you are a difficult man to fathom. Mysterious. And because of this you interest her."

Maria-Teresa emptied her glass. "Mysterious? *Hombre!* I think he's gorgeous."

I felt myself reddening and turned my back. I wasn't quite sure of my lines and felt stupid. Helena settled on the wing of the sofa and crossed her ankles. "Now you've embarrassed him."

Maria-Teresa blew me a kiss and came toward me taking

short steps like a geisha. "Have I embarrassed you, Señor-Inspector?"

"Not yet," I lied. The game they were playing was new to me and I had no idea of the rules. Instinct told me that one false assumption could land me in a lot of trouble.

She opened her eyes very wide and smiled, beating her palms together.

"Viva!" Her lips touched mine, then she led me across the room to the bottle of champagne. "More, please."

I filled her glass again. Helena smoothed a fold of her dress, her half-smile malicious. "Perhaps it won't be you who has his scalp after all. It could be Dolores."

Her sister's face sobered. "Dolores Beltrán? Aiee!" She looked at me thoughtfully. "Tell me, John. Would you like to be devoured by Messalina?"

"Absolutely not," I said. "But thanks for giving me the opportunity. Have you any idea how many people are going to be there tonight?"

They looked at one another. Maria-Teresa widened her hands. "Who knows?" she said indifferently. "They'll be coming from Jerez and Seville as well as Madrid. One hundred, two. What matters is that we shall be very, very late and enjoy ourselves. Do you promise you will try?"

I made a quick sign of assent. "I seem to remember you saying something about going back to Madrid with the Minister."

She glanced up from her hand mirror. "There will be many beautiful women. Jesus-Maria will probably spend the night there. We come home with you." She darkened the mole on the side of her nose.

The gun had lodged against my hip bone. I shifted it surreptitiously. "I wouldn't wish for anything better."

"Hah!" Helena uncrossed her ankles. "You may live to regret those words. I suppose you have been many times in front of film cameras?"

The question hung around my neck like a garland of flowers, a tribute to what was supposed to be my colorful past. I thought of my last night as Detective-Inspector Raven, the sound truck parked in Fulham Road, the three Poles behind the shabby-front restaurant.

"Only once," I said. "It was a kind of television interview. Nothing really very interesting."

Helena traced a pattern with the toe of her shoe. "Do you know these people well? Wolfie's friends, I mean. The Americans."

I made my tone as casual as hers. "I saw them for the first time the day before yesterday. You were there in the bar."

She turned the corners of her mouth down. "I thought it a little too much. A man wearing blue eye shadow. And in broad daylight. But I think the girl is quite pretty."

"So does she," Maria-Teresa's eyes narrowed. "What do you think they *do* together?"

It was an area that I no longer wanted to explore. "The mind boggles," I said. "Probably nothing. I imagine it's no more than a professional association."

A car snarled in the distance and the clatter of the Volkswagen was unmistakable.

Helena fished a speck from her glass with a varnished nail. "Pablo seems to like them but then I suppose they're his kind of people."

"Pablo likes Pablo," retorted her sister. "And by all accounts they are good at beating drums."

Helena consulted her watch. She picked a silk scarf from the back of the sofa, looked around at the disorder and shrugged.

"I think we'd better go."

We walked outside to the car. Someone had closed the door but the lights were left on and the windows open. It was no skin off my nose if they were robbed. Jewels for them, I suppose, were like men, easily replaceable. What needled me was that they had no right to flaunt their indifference to either.

Helena drove. There was enough room in the front of the Rolls for the three of us. I sat between them, deep in the white hide upholstery. They chatted away in Spanish, sudden explosions of words and then silence. A ton of expensive machinery glided down to the coastal highway. The lemon segment of moon pasted against the indigo sky shed its pale, fixed radiance on the ghostly stretch of bull pasture. We were fifteen miles past the turnoff to Villa Florida and going west in the direction of Jerez. The only traffic we met were a few Cádiz-bound trucks, their driving lights glowing in the distance. I kept my eyes on the silvered highway, thinking about what I'd said to George Ashley. The crack about *Alice in Wonderland* wasn't so wide of the mark. There was a sense of unreality in what I was doing, as if I'd stumbled unwittingly through a door into a world of total fantasy.

Maria-Teresa was sitting close to me. The movements of her body released wafts of Balenciaga. "We were talking about the Beltráns," she informed. "Dolores is sick — crazy."

Helena accelerated into the oncoming bend. "Crazy like a fox, the Americans say. Most of the time, she gets what she wants. This is not so sick."

I lifted my chin. "What about him? Is he as good a painter as he thinks he is?"

Her fingers fluttered on the wheel. "A genius! What else can you call a man who paints as he does?"

Maria-Teresa sniffed. "A confidence-trickster. A ringmaster in a circus. A madame in a nineteen-twenty brothel. Choose which you will but genius never!"

The car swung into the straight. Helena's voice was unmoved. "*Bueno*. The man is one thing, the painter another."

"The same person," retorted her sister. "A draftsman incapable of drawing anything from imagination. A dirty-minded *arriviste* who longs to be Picasso."

Helena's laugh tinkled like a Chinese glass screen. "Maria-Teresa posed for him in Mexico two years ago. In the nude. He amused himself in a very peculiar fashion. She has never forgiven him. We are almost there."

112

She braked and a road sign showed up ahead. CONVENTO DE CHRISTUS REY PROPIEDAD PARTICULAR. She forked left, heading the Rolls toward a cluster of lights that showed in the darkness beyond. Trees crowded the road, squeezing it into a narrow lane that ran between rough stone walls. We jolted past barns and cow sheds into a tiny village square. Four Civil Guard Land-Rovers were drawn up side by side. Guards were everywhere. It was well after eleven but no one in the village was sleeping. Every available space was crammed with spectators impelled by the frank curiosity of children. Fat women bulged over windowsills. Babies howled. Old men peered from doorways. Dogs relieved themselves furtively against the wheels of the Land-Rovers.

Helena cut the motor and lit a cigarette. Her features assumed a blend of arrogance and authority as an officer detached himself from a group of men. His patent leather hat gleamed above an immaculate uniform. He came over to the car and saluted courteously. Narrow black eyes flecked with brown scanned the interior of the car, then settled on the driver.

"Muy buenas, Señores. Dónde va?"

Helena pulled a card from her purse and showed it to him. He scanned it briefly and returned it. His eyes lingered on me. Another car drew up behind us. He saluted again and pointed across the square.

"Vaya con Dios, Señora!"

Helena selected the right gear and the Rolls whispered across the square. A woman hanging from a window beat her hands in applause. She was fifty, obese and wore a carnation behind her ear as if it was the most natural thing in the world. Looking at her, I could see that it was. We were traveling down another narrow lane with the headlamps picking out the sentinels stationed behind the walls. My voice sounded strained and unnatural.

"Correct me if I'm wrong but I had a distinct impression of being superfluous."

Maria-Teresa was busy with lipstick and mirror again.

"You mean the Civil Guard? There's nothing to worry about."

"Then why am I worrying?" I demanded.

She rolled her lips, consulting the mirror. "You're a foreigner with two Spanish-speaking women. No Spaniard likes that."

"But you're not Spanish," I objected.

She snapped her purse shut. "You are a man with two women and in Spain. That is two times more than enough, my friend."

Helena braked in front of wrought iron gates embellished with an ornate "B" surrounded by a gilded sunburst. The castellated walls of a fifteenth-century building towered over a courtyard where liveried servants were waiting. Fountains plumed, the colored, iridescent water cascading in the flood-lights. A pair of noctural peacocks stalked haughtily across the yard. A couple of men materialized from the shadows. They were identical in manner and appearance: squat, hatless and dressed in nondescript dark clothes. I knew the breed well. They were the ultimate expression of secret power, faceless and nameless except to one another. They lived in compounds, isolated from those they spied on. They married one another's sons and daughters. Because of them telephone calls were made in the dawn hours of morning, dossiers grew thicker by the inch, trusted voices whispered betrayal. They called themselves agents of the *Dirección General de Seguridad*.

They stationed themselves, one on each side of the car. Helena touched a button and her window rolled down. The man facing her held out his hand.

"*Carta, por favor!*"

Helena surrendered it with high dignity. He took the invitation card to the light and brooded over it like some evil bird of prey. Meanwhile his companion propped his weight against the convertible as if testing his ability to shift it bodily. The man was back, returning the card with fingers tipped by short square nails. He was looking at me. Details

114

impressed themselves on my mind. The way his bristle of hair shaped to a "V" at the front of his head, a grease spot on his lapel, the dead stonelike stare. The gun seemed to bulge in my cummerbund like a howitzer.

"*Y está Señor?*" he inquired.

Helena answered in metallic Spanish.

"*Pasaporte!*" he snapped.

I made a show of searching my pockets for what I knew wasn't there. I offered my driver's license.

"Tell him my passport's back at the club."

She spoke again, rapidly and without pause. The key words banged in my brain. *Inglés. Señor Beltrán. El Ministro.* He inspected me, his square nails scratching the cover of my driver's license. Then he returned it.

"*Vaya!*" he said indifferently. He lifted a hand and the wrought iron gates swung open.

8

THE ROLLS slid into the courtyard and the gates closed again. Maria-Teresa unfastened her door and climbed out, uncoiling like a leopard. The security men were checking the car that had followed us. The Rolls was driven away and Helena joined us. I gave an arm to each of them. Maria-Teresa's tone was curious.

"Your hand is shaking."

I looked down at her from what seemed to be a very great height. "And my legs have gone and I'm sweating. In fact I'm the perfect suspect."

She squeezed my arm. "They are only doing their job. Let's go inside."

A manservant wearing white cotton gloves was waiting just inside the entrance with a tray of champagne. We moved away with glasses. The enormous hall was timbered and vaulted and hung with emblazoned shields. Flambeaux licked the walls and ceiling with reddened light casting shadows on the faces of the people around us. Working on the Vice Squad I'd made a lot of strange arrests in my time. We once raided a house in Ascot and found eight grown men dressed as nuns. I've seen the insides of all those hookers'

117

pads in Shepherd's Market. But I'd never come face to face with this kind of thing. Most of the guests were young and dressed in Gatsby style. Men were wearing blond wigs and straight flapper dresses. Their Clara Bow mouths smiled from chalk white faces. The girls wore blazers and oxford bags, dinner jackets and shirts with wing collars and butterfly bows. Their eyes held us as we passed, then discarded us carelessly. Waiters with expressionless faces moved through the throng carrying trays of Scotch and champagne. Beltrán's legendary meanness with drink appeared to have been suspended for the occasion.

Helena had disappeared. I pressed on, guided by Maria-Teresa's touch on my elbow. Rooms opened on all sides. Couples were sprawling in deep sofas. Flowers blossomed in fireplaces and grew from an assortment of skulls. A trick mirror in a gilded empire frame distorted the faces of passersby. Music seeped from the walls, the Brazilian beat insistent. Maria-Teresa led me through a studded door into a stone-floored room empty of everything except a single painting on an easel. It was unframed and lit by a spotlight. The canvas was eight feet by six and represented three crucifixes. On two of these, girls were impaled upside down. Their long green hair hung to the ground and their mouths were smiling. Their breasts defied gravity, pointing to a white rabbit suspended on the cross between them. The rabbit's throat was cut and its glazed eyes were fixed on an apocryphal face in the skies above.

Maria-Teresa's heels clicked on the stone as she drew me to one side. "Look again!"

I did and as I looked, the blood on the rabbit's throat discongealed and began to flow and the glazed eyes rolled. I turned my head away, sickened. She pulled me, forcing me to look yet again, this time from a different angle. The blood stopped flowing and the eyes were dead. The effect was no more than a trick of light.

Her voice was quiet. "Beltrán. Well?"

I lit a cigarette and shrugged. The music stopped at the

doorway. In here it was cool and peaceful.

"What do you want me to say?"

"Whatever you feel."

I put the lighter back in my pocket. "I loathe it. If that's art I'll take *The Stag at Bay* any day. Let's get out of here." It was time I got rid of her and I'd no idea how to do it.

Her voice was the faintly regretful reflection of a woman who fears she had struck a bad bargain.

"Smile! These frowns are not becoming to you."

So I smiled. It seemed the only thing to do. We walked out to the corridor. It was lined with what looked like carved wood effigies of saints and martyrs. Closer inspection showed each statue to have the same features. Horse chestnut eyes floating in glycerine, a nose like a split pear over a pouting mouth, graying curls plastered against the lofty forehead. The expressions ranged from arch sanctity to sly resignation.

Maria-Teresa's tone was matter of fact. "And beyond that, he is a bore as well."

The corridor ended abruptly. I had never seen anything like the scene outside. Wide steps descended to a lawn the size of a football field. A thousand candles burned in the still air, laying a soft yellow patina over everything. Low tables had been set at the far end of the lawn. There were cushions to sit on instead of chairs. Carnations blazed against starched white napery. Three tall-capped chefs and their ruddy-faced helpers were sweating in front of charcoal grills. The air was pungent with the smell of roasting meat: beef, pork, pheasant. Maria-Teresa touched my sleeve and we walked down the steps and into the crowd. A table shaped like a horseshoe stood apart. Silver candelabra lit the array of bottles, coloring Scotch whisky peat brown, liqueurs green and yellow. I could see gin from England and Holland, schnapps from Germany, tequila from Mexico. Finnish and Polish vodka was embedded in solid blocks of ice. There was rum, bourbon and rye. The Brazilian music throbbed from the shadows beyond the lawn, sensual and sourceless. The trees behind were silhouetted in the moonlight, becoming part of the pageantry.

"*Hola!*" It was Maria-Teresa, looking up at me, wiggling her fingers. "Remember me?"

"I'm sorry," I said, smiling. "I've never seen anything quite like this before."

I followed her as she moved through groups of people, like silk rustling through calico. They were all transvestites and I searched for a face that I recognized. There was none. We climbed some steps to a pool where half a dozen lobsters were dying in the tinted saltless water. Maria-Teresa pushed into the throng at the end of the pool, leading me by the hand. She stopped in front of a man enthroned on a high tapestry-backed chair.

She spread her arms and genuflected, keeping her head erect. Her tone made a mockery of the greeting.

"Maestro!"

There was no mistaking the sliced-pear nose and sly convoluted eyes. Beltrán was wearing a toga made of barathea, Roman sandals and a plaited gold belt with a phallic clasp. He raised Maria-Teresa by the hand and pulled her close. His fingernails and toenails were painted silver and he was drunk. She made a face of disgust behind his back. Then he spun her like a dancer, displaying her to the woman by his side.

"*Mira,* Dolores. Maria-Teresa!"

His wife's hair was like freshly deposited seaweed and fell straight to her shoulders. It was cut in a bang over asphalt eyes, shiny but dead. She was closer to forty than thirty and had an old scar on her left cheek. A short beaded dress displayed beautiful legs and she wore no shoes. She looked at me from somewhere beyond the moon, her voice peculiarly vibrant. "*Hola, Maria-Teresa, qué tal?*"

Maria-Teresa kissed her cheek, groping behind for my hand. "This is John Raven. He is English and speaks no Spanish. Pablo and Dolores Beltrán."

Beltrán's grip was surprisingly firm. His English heavily accented.

"You are 'omosexual?"

Maria-Teresa answered for me. "No, he is not. Pablo likes to shock," she added.

The gun was bothering me again. No matter how I stood it was digging into my hipbone. I might have to find a temporary hiding place for it.

Beltrán's eyes rolled over me. "And you are not a painter?"

The faces behind us pressed toward the dialogue. "No," I said.

He snapped his fingers, one, two, three. "*Muy bien!* There *are* no English painters!" He waited for his laugh like a real ham before joining in.

Maria-Teresa poked her tongue out at him. "He is a poet."

"*Muy bien*," he said again. "The thoughts should always be free. Like a woman's breasts."

Maria-Teresa removed herself from his grasp. "You're drunk. Is Jesus-Maria here?"

Beltrán's face assumed a certain resentment. "Jesus-Maria? Not yet. But ministers are always late. It is necessary to their sense of importance."

I sneaked a look at the crowd below, looking for signs of Giselle or Wolfie. I could see no one. Beltrán closed his eyes for a moment as if hearing far-off sounds. He opened them again and belched.

"I am not afraid of God or ministers, Señor Englishman. They can kiss my arse. With Beltrán all is possible because my mind is pure. That is the great secret. How much do you know of television?"

"Not a thing," I answered.

He nodded approval. "It is a piece of shit. But I shall bring it form, dignify a primitive art form."

I floundered into my thank-you speech. "It's very good of you to have me here."

He waved a hand airily. "You are a nobody but this is not your fault. I sense humility in you. My wife will show you

121

my paintings. This one stays here.''

He made room on the chair for Maria-Teresa who clasped her hands in mock exultaion.

"What honor! What privilege!''

He pulled her down beside him. "You are prettier than your titless sister.''

His wife's thin smile razored and dismissed them both. She combed her hair like Lorelei and padded across to me on bare soles. Her basalt stare had the fixity of a cobra's.

"I will show you paintings.''

I barely heard her. My mind was on other things. Wolfie Field was standing no more than twenty yards away on the lawn below, talking to two people. His back was half-turned and he was waving his hands to emphasize the points he was making.

It was twenty minutes to midnight. I wanted Wolfie in my own time and in a place of my own choosing. My height made concealment difficult. I went down the steps behind Dolores Beltrán wishing that I could chop myself off at the knees. A waiter with a tray of drinks took Wolfie's attention. By the time his head turned round again we were safely under the cloisters. Dolores hung on to my hand as if the light, dry touch of her fingers was reading my pulse. She led me through the entrance hall, ignoring the few people who were loitering there, up the wide staircase, her eyes expressionless. The legs under the beaded dress were ten years younger than her face. She negotiated a couple of doors, her bare soles making a sandpaper noise on the carpet, and led me through a succession of passages to a remote wing of the convent. She stopped on a landing, opened another door and leaned against a wall brocaded in raised golden threads.

"Paintings!''

There were two of them, cunningly lit and framed. The first showed a tortured Christ with deliquescent flesh, clinging to the cross like molten lava. The second painting was larger, depicting a rotting haunch of venison infested with flies with Hieronymus Bosch faces. A plastic Sacred Heart was applied to the wall. A green button was below. She put her thumb on the button, activating a music box within the wall cavity. Her mimicry of her husband's voice and accent was perfect.

"In every hooman heart there is moosic!"

The box played the opening bars of *Eine kleine Nachtmusik*. "My husband cannot deny his genius," she said. I suddenly realized that she too was drunk. Either drunk or drugged. The pupils of her eyes were microdots in asphalt lakes.

"*Kitsch!*" she announced in a loud clear voice. "Shit and kitsch, all of it. Beltrán and his entourage."

A nearby door across the landing was open. The room was in darkness but enough light filtered in for me to see the white bearskin carpet and enormous bed. The only sound now was the echo of the music box.

Something about her manner made me feel nervous and I glanced at my watch. "Hadn't we better be getting back? I mean, this is an occasion for me. I wouldn't want to miss anything."

She dragged her hair from her face to see me better. "You mean the Ascension? Then you know about that."

I not only sounded embarrassed, I looked embarrassed. "Which Ascension is this?"

She smiled dreamily. "Beltrán's. Or perhaps it is the Assumption. Perhaps he has not made up his mind."

I skated off the thin ice hurriedly. "All this is a tremendous experience for me. I mean I've never seen anything like it. That's why I don't want to miss anything."

She leaned back against the wall, the movement lifting the beaded dress above her rounded knees. "What do you need in life, Señor Raven?"

I searched for my lighter, appreciating how an actor must feel on stage. It was difficult to know what to do with my hands.

"I've never really thought about it," I answered.

"*Tendresse?*" she suggested. "Human contact?"

"I suppose," I said. "Everybody needs that."

"Do you want to make love to me?" she said slowly.

A whole series of alarms sounded in my brain. Her eyes were completely blank. I met her empty stare head-on.

"No," I said frankly. I regretted it as soon as I'd spoken. The word, not the thought. What she was asking for was impersonal, a hand from a stranger.

She pushed her hair back again. She sounded confused rather than angry. "But you are not homosexual."

I blew smoke, wondering how to explain without sounding ridiculous. And getting nowhere with it.

"You're a very desirable woman. But I have to be emotionally involved."

Life flickered in her eyes. "You even *talk* like an Anglo-Saxon," she said bitterly.

"I'm sorry . . ." I started. But she didn't wait to hear but rushed past and ran down the stairs. By the time I reached the main part of the building she had vanished. I found my way out to the cloisters. The crowd on the lawn had pushed to the side of the pool. A snatch of conversation from a couple of French boy-girls in jeans established the reason. The Minister for Information and Tourism had arrived.

"You've no idea when they're going to start filming?" I asked in French.

They were no more than nineteen with the delicate eroticism of a Fragonard painting. Both seemed surprised to be addressed in their own language. The taller one answered.

"After we have eaten, I believe. So someone said. I saw people with cameras."

I walked in the direction of the pool, staying in the shelter of the cloisters. I'd forgotten about hiding the gun. Sixty yards on, some steps led up to a balcony. It faced south, high enough to catch whatever breeze there was. Abbesses must have sat there in the past, controlling the discipline of the novices in the gardens. I leaned over the parapet, in deep shadow and hidden from the people below. It was like being in a stage box, with the actors twenty feet beneath, diagonally off to my left. Beltrán was standing with his arm around Maria-Teresa, his laughter a bronze-lunged bellow of obscenity. Giselle Dale was there, workmanlike in shirt and jeans. I could see Abbott's blond head. He was wearing what looked like a Kung-Fu outfit, baggy-sleeved and trousered with a hand movie camera slung by a strap over his shoulder. Wolfie Field was in a group standing behind Beltrán. The object of everyone's attention was a man about my own age, one of the new breed of Spaniard, as big as a German with light brown hair and a silk suit cut in the Italian style. He had an attractive laugh and was talking to Giselle in nearly faultless English with the ease of a man who is used to words. I could hear him quite clearly.

"With Pablo Beltrán to perform, who needs the Minister for Information and Tourism?"

Laughter drowned Giselle's reply but I heard Abbott. "It's getting on to midnight. I thought if we could eat and start dancing I could get the background action I need for the Ascension."

Beltrán nodded vigorously, dislodging the laurel wreath on his head. "I shall take off my clothes!" He moved forward to the steps, banging his hands in the air for attention. *"Vamos comer! La comida, amigos!"*

I watched them across the lawn, Beltrán leading the way, holding his wife's hand. Maria-Teresa and the Minister were deep in conversation. Behind them came Giselle and Abbott with Wolfie Field's white suit prominent among the blazers, the 1920 dinner jackets and kooky costumes. It was a buffet meal, the guests collecting their food from the serving tables.

A light in the cork oaks beyond the lawn drew my attention. Someone was signaling with a flashlight. Another flash answered immediately, from a point twenty yards away. Then another and another till the cryptic signals ringed the convent as far as I could see. The woods were thick with security men, armed certainly and probably with dogs. There was only one road in and out of the place and I still had no idea what Giselle and her playmates had in mind. In fact I was beginning to wonder whether the whole thing wasn't some sort of ghastly joke being played out at my expense. I kept coming back to Dolores Beltrán's reference to her husband's Ascension. That was why Christian was missing. They were going to use the helicopter and for all I knew film Beltrán being trailed through the night climbing to the undercarriage. Nothing was too fanciful or indeed too ridiculous. I sneezed hard, asking myself what I was doing at midnight with a case of hay fever coming on and a loaded gun in my possession.

The music had changed to hard rock with a pounding beat that came out of the speakers decibels louder. I was halfway down the steps to the food when a light came on behind the pool, glowing like the birth of a sunrise. Red tinged to orange then to soft molten gold revealing a marble dance floor. At the moment of full revelation fireworks burst from the roof of the convent, spinning and wheeling in a myriad of color. Explosions rattled and a loud whoosh carried a rocket skyward. It hung in the night for a second, then dissolved into fire-streaked characters spelling out the words ¡VIVA MAESTRO!

The tribute disintegrated, leaving only the smell of exploded gunpowder. The candles shivered in a silence broken by the thudding rock rhythm. Hands clutching plates of smoked salmon and vodka glasses seemed frozen. The faces of their owners, some wearing Clockwork Orange make-up, turned towards Beltrán's table. Someone shouted and the silence dissolved into chatter and laughter. Toasts were raised as Beltrán lurched upright, his glass high over his head. I slipped along the corridor and joined the throng around the serving table, keeping well away from Abbott and company. My appetite was nil but I covered a plate with salad and roast pheasant, keeping the lowest profile possible in the shifting crowd as I took my food to a nearby table. A cushion was free and I squatted awkwardly, hidden from the Beltrán group by a forest of candlesticks and wine bottles. I poured myself a glass of red, watching my neighbors from the corners of my eyes. They all seemed to be paired or together. Nobody spoke to me. I kept my head down, the plate of food in front of me untouched, smoke curling from the cigarette between my fingers. I was aware that people came and went, that sorbets, ice cream and fruit arrived. A crop-haired girl sitting across from me in a striped gangster's suit slowly subsided, her overturned glass flooding the tablecloth. A fat man dressed as Mae West rose with difficulty and struggled her toward the house.

The glow surrounding the dance floor dissolved into temporary darkness and the music grew louder. New lights came on, harsh, bright and angled, forming a psychedelic pattern that completely destroyed perspective. Couples started making for the floor. I heaved myself up, crossed the lawn to the cloisters and went up the steps to the balcony. There was a faint breeze that carried the scent of jasmine, causing the candles below to draw breath and then flame again. It was twenty minutes to one. I had a good view of Beltrán's table. He was haranguing his guests, flinging his arms around as he talked. I could see Maria-Teresa with the Minister's mouth close to her ear, the flash of Wolfie's white suit, Giselle next to him.

I searched for Abbott and found him standing on a chair by the edge of the pool. He had his movie camera trained on the dance floor where a crowd surrounded a young man wearing a long blond wig. Other than that he was completely naked and gyrating to the music with his eyes closed. Following the beat, he went into a rapid succession of bumps and grinds, then sank to the floor in the manner of Nureyev, arms outstretched and wig askew. The music stopped to prolonged applause and Beltrán rose to acknowledge it. The people at his table followed him across the lawn, Giselle dabbing at his face with what looked like a powder puff. Finished with him, she planted herself in front of the Minister and repeated the process. Abbott panned his camera as both men came up the steps. Amateur photographers were recording the scene, flash bulbs popping. Someone went over backward to join the lobsters in the pool. A girl shrieked.

A movement of something white caught my eye. It was Wolfie Field detaching himself from the scene at the pool and heading for the house. I ran down the steps and along the cloisters. Trail of cheroot smoke guided me down the corridor to a cloakroom. I was somewhere near the kitchens. I could hear voices and the clattering of crockery. I tried the doorhandle, turned it gently and stepped inside.

Wolfie's red-lined jacket was hanging on a hook, his cheroot smoldering in an ashtray. He was leaning forward with his head immersed in a bowl of cold water. He came up, eyes closed and spluttering as he reached for the towels on the shelf. I moved past him, grabbed a towel and placed it in his outstretched hand. His eyes opened immediately and his reflection stared back at me from the mirror. He looked shocked.

"Jesus Christ!" he said with feeling. "What the hell do you think *you're* doing here?"

I slipped the gun from my waistband. "This thing's properly loaded now, Wolfie. They tell me if I pull the trigger anything can happen. I don't want to do it but if I have to I will."

His face was slowly regaining its normal color. He mopped the water from his face and threw the damp towel at the basket.

"There was no guy in Cádiz, right?"

"Right," I said steadily. Someone turned the doorhandle. I used the key before the door opened.

He leaned back, his hands on the edge of the basin. "Okay, so you've got more tricks than a Montreal hooker but this time your arse is on the line. This place is crawling with cops. Who do you think you are, Batman? They find you with that gun and they'll blow you away without asking one single question."

I was genuinely shocked at his deceit. It was like pulling a thorn from a dog's paw and getting bitten in the arse.

He turned his back on me again and started combing his

hair. The shake in his hands was transmitted to his shoulders.

"I don't think you understand," I said. "I've been putting things together, Wolfie. You and I have done a few laps in the past. This caper isn't your style, it's out of character. What have they got on you?"

He emptied the water in the bowl, his fingers still jittery. "You look ridiculous with that thing stuck in your hand. What are trying to do to me, Raven?"

"I'm trying to stop you from making a fool of yourself," I answered.

He slipped into the red-lined jacket and adjusted the handkerchief in the pocket. Then he turned to face me again. "Trying to stop *me* from making a fool of myself. I can see quite clearly where you're going to be a big pain in the arse."

The person outside rapped on the door. I looked past the mask of confidence to the certainty behind. "You loaded this gun with blanks, Wolfie. Then as soon as you thought I was safely out of the way, you ran for your friends. I want to know why."

He relit the dead cheroot and lowered his voice. "There's no time for whys and wherefores, Raven. You and I owe one another nothing. But I'll level with you. Get yourself out of here as fast as you can. I mean *now*. And I'll guarantee that your passport's back in your possession before nine o'clock tomorrow morning. Don't ask why, just do it."

I waved the gun barrel from side to side, hoping I looked more impressive than my reflection in the mirror. "You've got it the wrong way round, Wolfie. I'm supposed to be the one who gives the orders. You've got thirty seconds to answer my question. *Why?*"

"And if I don't answer?" His eyes locked on mine.

I shrugged. "I get carried away with my own production."

He blew a cloud of smoke reflectively. "Suppose I told you I was in love, that I'm up there without wings and no engine. You don't have to tell me I'll crash. I already know it."

I stared at him in disbelief. "In love with *whom?*"

When he raised his head, his eyes were curiously remote.
"Giselle Dale."

I shook my head slowly. "I'm going to say this as pleasantly as I can. If what you've just told me is true you've got no chance at all."

His expression was stony. "I'm the happiest man in the world," he said. His fingers found the light switch as he spoke and the cloakroom went dark. I ducked instinctively, swinging away from him but his aim was shrewd. His foot exploded between my legs and I fell to my knees, grabbing at my balls with both hands.

"On your feet," Wolfie said from the darkness. Then the light came on again.

I had dropped the gun and now he had it. Someone banged on the door, this time harder. A voice called in Spanish.

"*Momento,*" yelled Wolfie. He showed his teeth at me like Bogart being last man out of some waterfront bar.

I was seeing everything through a pain-induced haze, bent over like an old man and ready to vomit. Wolfie brought his face close to mine. It was a new face, tense, committed and totally menacing.

"You had your chance," he said in a savage whisper. "So don't crowd me."

He slipped the gun into his jacket pocket and kept his hand there. He used the other one to open the door. A plump Spaniard in spangles and wearing a Che Guevara mustache eyed us suspiciously. Wolfie flashed him a friendly smile, nodding at me and lifted an imaginary glass to his mouth.

"*Demasiado de vino.*"

He wrapped an arm around my shoulder and led me tenderly along the corridor. The gun in his pocket was digging into my kidney. My body was drenched with sweat and my mouth was hanging open like a goldfish's. He urged me on into a shambling run. A great roaring filled the air as we came out of the cloisters. People were running across the lawn, pointing up into the sky. The chutter-chutter sound grew louder. The helicopter came in low over the cork oak trees, a giant mosquito with a single searchlight eye. It hovered near the swimming pool, thirty feet above the ground.

We neared the stone wall that formed the side of the raised pool. Wolfie jammed me up against it. The light on his face was reflected from the colored water.

"Fuck me up and I'm going to kill you, Raven," he warned.

The pain in my groin was intense but I was standing a little straighter. The helicopter was settling in front of the steps. Abbott was still up on his perch, filming its descent. The noise of the engines was deafening. The candles went out. Skirts, hair and napkins ballooned in the sudden rush of air. A scarf sailed overhead and vanished. Beltrán and the Minister were up above us at the end of the pool. I could see Giselle behind them with some kind of make-up bag. She showed no sign of nerves but her eyes were everywhere. Wolfie bunched my sleeve in his fist and tugged it gently.

"Am I coming through to you?"

It was an effort to nod but I managed it. "This woman's going to ruin you, Wolfie."

"Sure," he said.

Strange how illogical emotions can be. This man had just kicked me in the balls and was threatening to kill me. And here I was feeling sorry for him. He'd come a long way from nowhere, a natural scoundrel yet one with integrity.

I pulled my sleeve from his grasp. "You're not going to kill me, Wolfie."

"Don't make a book on it," he cautioned.

"Giselle *Dale*," I said. "Jesus Christ. You know something, I've just this second realized what this is all about. You're insane, Wolfie. It's not your scene. Why don't you walk away from it now, with me?"

"I can't." He shook his head. "Just do as you're told and you won't get hurt, Raven."

I wiped the sweat from my forehead. "I've got a lot of things left in life to do. So tell me."

The twin engines stopped simultaneously, leaving the

music playing to an empty dance floor. A cabin door opened and Christian's head appeared. The harness with speaker and earphones gave him the appearance of some nightmare insect from a land where genes had run wild. He leaned out of the cabin yelling across at Abbott.

"Tell them to get the fuck away, can't you!"

Abbott walked forward, waving his arms. The crowd retreated, leaving Wolfie and me standing close to the stone retaining wall. The space above us, at the end of the pool, was a natural proscenium. The only people there were the Minister and Beltrán, Giselle and Abbott. Christian swung the searchlight round, training it on them. Giselle flapped his powder puff over the principals' faces and stepped out of range. Abbott panned the camera from one man to the other. His tanned face was smiling as he came to the top of the steps.

"Hands up all those who understand English!"

Hands went up. He shaded his eyes, looking out over the crowd on the lawn. "Okay, people, this is your big moment."

"Yours too," Wolfie said quietly. I felt the weight of the gun being pressed into my side. I was shaking and there was nothing that I could do about it.

Abbott signaled to the audience, his Kung-Fu tunic billowing as he moved. "I want you all standing well back. Come on, further yet! Okay, now listen. I'm going to be in the helicopter with the camera. It's the Maestro's Ascension and you're all deeply affected. The moment we lift off I want you running after us, looking up into the sky. I want emotion— joy, rapture and tears!" He turned to Beltrán. "Tell them in Spanish."

The painter stepped forward like a diva acknowledging what she knows to be just applause. He was drunk and his bulging eyes focused with difficulty. The Minister was a contrast behind him, a study in elegant aloofness. I could see his smile thin as Beltrán picked a wine bottle from the ground. The painter put his head back and poured straight from the neck into his open mouth. He threw the empty bottle into the pool, wiped his lips on the hem of his toga and started his harangue.

Wolfie leaned forward, beckoning Giselle over. She squatted on her heels in front of us. I was close enough to smell her scent, to see the pulse in her throat. She turned her eyes on me as he whispered in her ear. She nodded and walked back to Abbott, smiling at the Minister as she went. Abbott listened as she relayed the news. My body seemed drained of strength, my mind of volition. If I'd had the chance I'd have dropped where I was and let the bastards walk over me.

Beltrán came to the end of his speech and waddled forward, raising his arms. *"Aplauso!"* he shouted.

There was a dutiful rattle of handclaps. A few cheers. A woman in Turkish trousers plucked a flower from her dyed ginger hair and tossed it in his direction.

"El Divino!"

Christian had opened both cabin doors. I could see his face behind the perspex screen, his eyes on the scene at the top of the steps.

We are nearing the dénouement. "Action!" called Giselle. Abbott turned, holding a heavy hand-camera steady. Alatren and Beltran went into an embrace, the painter's pear-shaped nose barely reaching the Minister's shoulder. Shouts of approval greeted the performance. Giselle walked over to us. Her bare brown breasts swung as she leaned forward smiling down at Wolfie. She spoke for the benefit of the people standing behind us, her voice relaxed as if the instruction was some integral part of the script.

"Now if you two would like to get aboard . . ."

Wolfie jerked his head. We started walking toward the helicopter. My feet seemed to drag across the grass. I could hear the voices plainly but the faces in the crowd were painted balloons. I thought I was going to vomit. The pain between my legs had returned. A girl laughed as I stumbled. Wolfie hoisted me up into the cabin. I fell into the seat behind the pilot, with Wolfie at my side. Giselle and Abbott were backing down the steps, Abbott grinding the camera as Beltrán and the Minister followed. I twisted sideways suddenly, summoning strength for a cracked shout that echoed back from the cloisters. "Police! Help!"

Wolfie's forearm snaked about my neck, throttling me. I felt my eyes protruding as the pressure increased, the veins sticking out in my forehead. My legs thrashed uselessly. Somebody screamed as a gun jumped from the make-up box into Giselle's hand. A flurry of bodies sent Beltrán sprawling. Abbott grabbed the Minister and ran him across the grass, Giselle close behind covering them. The Navaho hit the starters as they climbed into the helicopter. The last thing I saw was Beltrán up on his feet and staggering. He was shaking his fist, tears of rage in his eyes.

"Y Yo, *hijos de putas! Y* Yo, *Beltrán?*"

The doors slammed and the helicopter lifted vertically, defying gravity under the powerful thrust of its twin motors. Suitcases in the cargo hold slithered across the floor as the craft altered its pitch.

Wolfie's weight jammed me against the side of the cabin. He smelled strongly of Cuba libres which explained his activities in the loo earlier on. Our new course provided a tilted view of the terrain below. The convent lay serene in the moonlight. A line of curling surf marked the edge of the ocean. The police vehicles were toys in the tiny square. All hell must have been breaking loose down there but from where we were everything looked peaceful. The helicopter chopped its way westward through the night, climbing toward the spangle of stars. I wriggled myself free of Wolfie's weight, massaging my throat where he'd as good as mugged me. The farther up we climbed, the brighter the moonlight seemed. The instrument panel was a glow of dials. I could hear the static and voices in Christian's earphones.

Abbott took the heavy Walther automatic from Giselle, and checked the clip professionally; they both considered us. By us I mean the Minister, Wolfie and me. She, twisted round and resting her chin on the back of the seat; he, from the far side of Don Jesus-Maria. Abbott's free hand trailed over the movie camera in the cargo compartment behind us. He smiled over at Wolfie.

"Raven's no problem, right?" His voice was sarcastic.

The Kung-Fu outfit and blue eye-shadow failed to make him ridiculous. Insanity can't be ridiculous and there was something definitely unbalanced in the way that he smiled.

"You scored, didn't you?" Wolfie said shortly.

Abbott nodded. "Know something, Wolfie, I had an idea that you'd be the one to fuck up."

"Let him alone," said Giselle. "I don't like you sticking my friends in a corner."

Wolfie's gun was in his lap. I saw his finger crook around the trigger. One shot and we'd all be riding on the wind. "Respect," he said. "You know how I like respect."

Christian pushed up his earphones. His voice was petulant. "Anyone want to remember what *I* said about Raven? I said lose him down there." He took a hand off the stick, stabbing a finger at the black vastness of the ocean on our left.

I fumbled for a cigarette, making each movement obvious but nobody stopped me. Giselle stroked the back of Christian's neck. "You just drive, baby. Everything's going to be all right." She adjusted the earphones on his head and rested her chin on the back of the seat again.

The noise of the engines had become part of my hearing. Small sounds crept in, registering in my brain. The hiss of air along the fuselage, my own breathing. The Minister was sitting up straight, legs crossed, eyes closed.

"I told him about us." It was Wolfie speaking to Giselle.

She shook her head vaguely. "Once in the Dear Dead Days Beyond Recall . . ." she sang. Her singing voice was half a tone flat. "That was wrong, darling. You see, there's this girl who committed suicide. Two hits of Lebanese Gold and I reminded him of her. In a way it was touching."

I looked at her steadily. "You're an evil bastard. You really are."

Wolfie's mouth went white but she just pouted. "But we

made it together, Inspector! Don't worry about Wolfie. He's not the possessive type and anyway you came in the line of duty, so to speak.''

She was goading him as well as me, completely sure of herself and in any case riding a high that put her beyond reason. Both she and Abbott had been smoking.

I tongued my courage into my mouth. "*Look* at her, Wolfie! This bitch is going to take your eyeteeth and sink them into your brain. *Look* at her!"

He turned his head slowly and looked at me instead. He knew and didn't care. It was as simple as that. She laughed and Abbott laughed. The Minister kept his eyes closed and Wolfie just stared at me. Then the Minister opened his eyes. He was big enough to have taken Abbott and showed no fear. In fact he might have been speaking in the comfort of his own drawing room.

"Who are you?" he asked quietly. "What do you want from me?"

Abbott was playing with the gold fish slung around his neck. "I thought you'd never ask. We are Reinforcements for Revolution."

The engines droned on. We were flying at a hundred twenty miles an hour, a thousand feet above sea level.

Don Jesus-Maria's handsome face appeared interested. "Perhaps you would explain."

It sounded all too familiar to me. Political naifs who are prepared to lead a life of violence if necessary, an intense life expecting nobody to mourn their failure or applaud their success.

It was Giselle who answered and what she said proved me right. She spoke as if she had recited the same thing over and over again.

"We are an autonomous movement without political label and our purpose is the establishment of a society based on need not greed. We have no leader, no followers, no head or tail, no affiliations."

"You mean you're *it?*" I couldn't help myself.

"That's right," said Abbott. "We're it, the three of us."

Don Jesus-Maria nodded courteously. Relaxed as he seemed I noticed that his eyes slid constantly sideways, looking out at the night.

"You have only answered half my question," he said. "What is it you want from me?"

Christian brushed up his headset again. His voice and face were excited. "I'm getting a whole lot of shit that I don't understand. I think it's the Spanish Air Force base at Huelva."

Wolfie grabbed the earphones, staring ahead through the perspex screen as he listened. He handed the headset back. "They've made us on radar."

"Fuck," said Abbott. The Minister crossed his arms and closed his eyes again. There was a little smile on his lips as if he'd just remembered something amusing.

"Gun it," said Wolfie. He turned to me, his face thin with menace. "One wrong move and I'll put you through the door."

He craned past me, looking at the growing lights below. They clustered on both sides of a silvered serpentine strip. "Ayamonte," he said. "It's the frontier — the Guadiana River. That's Portugal in front of us."

Christian put the helicopter into a long dive. It shuddered as he fed the engines more gas. We wheeled away from a hotel perched on a hill overlooking the town and down almost to the surface of the dark wide river. The rushes shivered as we approached the far bank, then we started to climb again. The lights of Spain receded in the distance. A compass on the panel showed that we were flying due north. Christian grinned into the rearview mirror.

"Say it's true! I'm the Original Birdman."

"You're a fucked-up little papoose," retorted Abbott. "How far off are we now?"

Christian checked his instruments. "About twenty minutes. And we're fifteen miles inside the border."

The news did nothing for my peace of mind. There was no

hope of help down there. From what I'd heard there hadn't been law or order in Portugal since the events of April 25, 1974. The defenders of western values in Africa had been betrayed by a clown with a riding crop and a monocle. A junta of Communist-trained army and navy officers had decreed themselves a permanent part of government and the most powerful civilian in the country was a cabinet minister back from exile in Russia.

Tree-covered hills repeated themselves in the moonlight below. Tenseness emanated from Wolfie. The others seemed to be floating in varying conditions of euphoria. I fished for another cigarette. The pack was nearly empty and God alone knew where the next would come from. Abbott's arm snaked in front of the Minister and Wolfie, offering me a light.

"Thanks," I said.

He looked at me with sudden interest. "You're sweating and that's uncool for a cop."

"You are a policeman?" The Minister's interest was as lively as Abbott's.

"I was," I said. "I seem to have lost the touch."

Giselle hung over the back of her seat, her chin on her hands.

"Can you ever forget that slob, Beltrán? 'Y Yo?' he kept shouting. He actually wanted to *be* in the helicopter!"

The Minister lit a cigarette from mine. There was something comforting in the thought that he too smoked Ducados. His hands were perfectly steady. His clothes and shoes showed the attention of a well-trained manservant and he was wearing some kind of decoration in the lapel of his silk jacket. His tone was quietly insistent.

"I must demand that you return me to Spanish territory. This is an outrage to my government!"

Christian had been watching in the small mirror. He flipped up the headset.

"What did he say?"

Giselle interpreted. "He said it's an outrage."

Christian gave Don Jesus-Maria the finger. "Darleenk!"

"Keep your mind on your job," drawled Abbott. He inclined his body toward the girl. "I told you he was cool, baby. I don't think he really understands this shit that we're putting down."

Water gleamed a thousand feet below. The rotor blades chopped on relentlessly. The airspeed indicator said we were doing one hundred twenty-five miles an hour. The concrete fall of a dam was bone white in the moonlight. The Spaniard looked at Christian with two thousand years of cold contempt.

"What is it that you people want of me?"

Abbott giggled, batting his blue-greased eyelids. "Well, it's like this, Excellency. You represent what's called a symbol of barter. There are six men and a woman sitting under sentence of death, right?"

Don Jesus-Maria's expression was unmoved. "Condemned after a full trial by a military tribunal. Murderers."

Giselle switched her head from side to side reprovingly. For a moment I thought it was me she was looking at but it was Wolfie.

"Do you see what I mean?" she demanded. "A full trial by military tribunal. *You* bang on about justice. Have you any idea what a military tribunal *is?* You're dead before you hear the charge."

"There is right of appeal," Don Jesus-Maria said stiffly. "It has been exercised."

She wasn't listening to him. "Well say something," she challenged Wolfie.

He stared back at her, licking his lips. There was little left of the Wolfie that I had known. I tried to tell myself that I understood but I didn't.

"I've come this far," he said in a determined sort of way. "I won't let you go now."

"You're a big disappointment to me," said Abbott from behind a raised finger. "You're a very selfish man. Your whole life's been one big ripoff, yet here you are like our friend, a fascist at heart."

Wolfie grinned and this time he was sure of himself. "Suppose I tell *you* something, Jerry. Reinforcements for Revolution, *shit!* You're nothing but a punk. This time next week this clown at the controls will be paddling in his oil field and Giselle and I will be married. What are you going to do, Jerry, all by yourself? It's cold out there."

"Married?" Abbott's mouth was supercilious. "The happiest man in the world, right?"

"Right," said Wolfie. "Half a million dollars and the woman I love. How about you, sweetheart?"

Giselle stroked Abbott's blond curls. "Jerry's going to be all right. He's young and beautiful."

"He's a punk," Wolfie repeated.

She was all things to all men and reasonable to the Minister. She spoke to him as if to a friend.

"I know a lot about you. I made it my business. Your father was an army colonel killed in the Civil War. You went to school in Switzerland, graduated from Barcelona University and you're a real live swinger. Your mother's a good friend of Donna Carmen's and you're smart. Now how much do you know about me?"

The Minister looked for an ashtray. Wolfie took the butt from him. Don Jesus-Maria half-smiled.

"That is easy to answer, Señorita, I know nothing of people like you except this — you cannot possibly win."

Frownmarks creased her forehead. "The old Bob Hope war cry! Let me tell you something about winning, my friend. You concentrate on one battle and no more. We've spent almost two years preparing for this one, just the three of us. No help from anyone else. And when it's over, we're going to walk away from one another and lead brand new lives. No looking back, no returns to take a bow. Just the curtain. And we'll have done more for revolution in one hit than all those dudes running around with bombs."

Liar that she was, I wanted to see her face but Wolfie's shoulder was in the way. Don Jesus-Maria uncrossed his legs.

"You said you had no political affiliations. These people you talk about, the ones under sentence of death, they are Trotskyites."

"We're broad-minded," said Abbott. "We dish it out where we think it's most needed."

I returned to a previous thought. The Navaho had a history of mental disturbance and stoned or not the other two were very close to it.

The helicopter banked and then straightened, the stars resuming a familiar pattern. Don Jesus-Maria spoke from a tight proud face.

"You make a strange choice. Your friends committed mass murder, eighteen innocent people destroyed, four of them children."

"Bullshit," said Abbott. "How about Guernica?"

The Minister's skin flushed under the tan. "What do you know of Guernica? I can tell you this: before we could only chop off the tentacles, now we have the head. My government will never surrender it."

Giselle and Abbott smiled at one another. It was Wolfie who answered for them as if he had been thinking about it for far too long.

"You'd just better hope that they do, Minister. You'd better hope that they do."

The helicopter swung into another arc. Christian peered down through the window. He had tied his long black hair behind his head like a hunting brave. Moonlight lay on sleepy white villages set among vast yellow cornfields. He showed us a thumb.

"The Red Baron flies again! It's the Alentejo. Ten more minutes and we're home."

Giselle smoothed her lips with the tip of her finger. It was a provocative ploy, an exercise in sensuality, aimed at Wolfie and me. I'll never know what made me say it. The words were out of my mouth before I thought.

"This whore's going to ruin you, Wolfie."

The flat of the gun landed against my cheekbone, splitting

my head in two. Every tooth in my head felt as it it had been shattered. A trickle of blood found its way down my cheek. I looked at it on my fingers, surprised that there was so little.

The sound of Giselle's voice cleared my head. "Let him talk, Wolfie. He's jealous."

My mind hurdled back to the only other time I'd been slugged with a gun. It had been a foggy night with the gangway leading to the houseboat slippery. Limehouse Nights weather. I'd walked up the gangway carefully. Some tear-away had been waiting on deck with a sawed-off shotgun. The first blast had torn a hole in the fog. It turned out that the man had been drinking for two hours. When his shotgun jammed he tried to use it as a club. I did my best to run but my legs refused the message. It was Holy Elmer who saved me. This was in the days when my one-eyed Doberman hadn't taken to accepting poisoned meatballs from strangers. The thing is that I'm not really made for violence.

I wiped my cheek with my handkerchief. "That makes twice, Wolfie."

His voice held a thin thread of warning. "I've had enough of your brainstorms, Raven. The third time's going to be for keeps."

Abbott looked back from the window. "They're a couple of inferior fuckers, Giselle, they really are! Brawling and stuff. I don't know what we're all coming to!"

He lurched with the rest of us as the aircraft slipped sideways. Christian's hand jabbed at the void beneath. "There it is. Veteran pilot brings crippled plane home safely."

"Duh-duh-duh," said Abbott and stuck his fingers up. My cheek was swelling and oozing blood. Wolfie hadn't looked at me since his outburst. The moon's pale clear light revealed whitewashed farm buildings huddled at the bottom of a small hill topped by a windmill. A stream fringed with willows meandered through shoulder-high corn. Flour sacks had been spread out in an "X" in front of a barn.

"Hang in there," warned Christian. "We're going down."

A giant shadow on the ground reproduced our flight. We dropped swiftly leaving my stomach five hundred feet up in the air. The Minister was sitting bolt upright, arms folded across his chest like a beginner in a riding school. The helicopter settled gently. Christian took off his headset and shook his hair free, smiling at Giselle.

"Beautiful, baby," she told him.

Abbott opened the door on his side and looked out. The windmill up on the hill stood like a gallows, etched against the false dawn staining the sky to the east. Barns and outbuildings flanked the low stone-built farmhouse. I could smell pigs. Nothing moved. Giselle swung her long legs over the side and sat there swinging them.

"On the banks of the Wabash far away," she said.

Christian jumped to the ground. He was wearing a suit of coveralls with an oil company emblem on the breast pocket. He cupped his mouth with his hands and let out a long low whistle. God alone knows why. Nobody within a mile could have missed the racket we made coming down. I heard the pigs grunting in one of the barns.

Giselle glanced up over her shoulder, swinging her hair. "I've got a feeling that the Red Baron goofed. Nobody's here," she said.

Everybody watched as Christian walked into the shadows veiling the outbuildings, holding up his hand. The door on my side of the cabin was open and Wolfie's back was to me. My left eye was half-closed and a dull ache still split my legs but I knew I could run. The thing was, *where?* I remembered a television documentary made in New Zealand about the sportsmen there who chased deer in the mountains, hunting them down with high-velocity rifles. I remembered the terror of the beasts as they galloped along the rock-faced trails pursued by helicopters. If I ran, these people would do the same thing to me, track me through these endless cornfields until the searchlight finally found me. Then they'd sling me to the undercarriage and drop me out at sea as promised.

I sneaked a look at my watch. It was after three. Another fourteen hours before George Ashley telephoned Scotland

Yard. I don't know why but I thought of the houseboat. A couple of Monday Club members who worked in a paint shop were doing the *Albatross* over after hours. I wondered if the paint would be dry by the time I got home.

9

Jerry Abbott slipped past Giselle and padded after the Navaho, the pistol hanging loosely in his hand. A door opened in the side of the barn as the two men neared it. The first person out was a bushy-bearded youngster wearing an elastic headband. He was holding a submachine gun with both hands like a professional, waist-high and arms stiff. He came through the doorway, dragging his left foot a little. The woman behind was dressed in black ill-fitting trousers and wore a stocking cap on the back of her head. She was no more than thirty, wide in the wrong places and her spectacles were big and square. They were about fifteen yards from the helicopter and I could see that she, too, was carrying a pistol, a revolver.

Abbott and Christian stopped dead as she raised it. "You will surrender your weapon," she said to Abbott. Her Cockney accent came as a surprise.

Abbott handed the weapon to the machine gunner, butt first. The woman turned to Christian.

"*Viva!*" I had the feeling that they knew one another.

"*Hola*, Luisa!" he said. He waved his arm at us, his teeth

flashing white against his dark skin. "We brought you a present!"

She glanced from Abbott to Giselle and then back to Christian. Standing close to the Indian she was even shorter than I thought. Her spectacles came level with his chest.

"I heard," she answered. "The news is splashed all over the short-wave band. Congratulations."

I'd been exposed to the same sort of voice a thousand times, snapping at me in public transport, reproving me at the other end of the phone.

"A tiny little fuck-up," Christian said, still smiling. He seemed to be pleased with himself and confident. "It altered our schedule but the main thing is that we delivered." He craned over her head, calling across to the helicopter. "Okay, Wolfie!"

Giselle let her feet down and sauntered toward the group by the barn. It was a challenge directly at the Portuguese woman and one that Luisa couldn't handle. Wolfie nudged the Minister. Don Jesus-Maria clambered down out of the cabin. He took a deep breath and then walked forward, head high. The bearded man collected Wolfie's weapon as he passed. No one had told me to move. I was still sitting in my seat nursing the faint hope that somehow I had been forgotten. Luisa's question put me right.

"Who's that?"

Wolfie signaled me out of the helicopter. I waddled a little but it was easier to walk than I'd imagined. Luisa's eyes searched my face.

"Who are you?"

I removed the handkerchief from my cheekbone. "John Raven."

The sickly sweet smell of pigs drifted out from the barn behind us. Nobody spoke. Luisa was still looking at me.

"No weapon?" she said after a while.

I shook my head. "No weapon."

"Think of him as another hostage," Christian said easily. "The others are with me. Giselle and Jerry you've heard about. Wolfie's a good friend of ours.''

She took the introductions coolly. ''You were supposed to bring a package. Where is it?''

Abbott clapped his hand to his forehead. ''God damnit, the scag! I almost forgot.''

He walked back to the helicopter, rummaged in the cargo hold and reappeared carrying a blue canvas overnight bag.

''Safe and sound,'' he said, holding the bag in the air.

We all moved toward the thick-walled farmhouse, the man with the machine gun bringing up the rear. The door slammed behind us. I heard the two bolts being rammed home. It was a long room with a ceiling made of varnished reeds. Down the middle was a rough oak table set with solid square-backed chairs. Religious prints decorated the unpapered walls. The doors to the adjoining rooms were made of raw wood. A complicated-looking radio squatted at the far end of the table, connected to heavy-duty storage batteries in the enormous fireplace. The lamps flickered constantly and I guessed that power was generated by the windmill on the hill.

The bearded man dragged a chair in front of the entrance and cradled his machine gun in his lap. He was chewing a piece of gum, his eyes fixed on Giselle. It was hard to tell with the beard but he was student age, in his late teens or early twenties. He was wearing a cloth dog tag outside his high-necked sweater and his headband was patterned with Aztec symbols.

Luisa pulled back the chair at the head of the table and sat behind the radio. She indicated our places. Jesus-Maria on her right, next to me. Abbott on her left, then Giselle and finally Christian. Luisa poked her gun into her blouse with a glimpse of shiny satin bra. She lit the smallest smoke I'd ever seen. The name on the pack was Kentucky, twelve for one escudo. Abbott lifted the blue canvas bag onto the table. His eye shadow was smeared but it hadn't destroyed his self-assurance.

''*Vosse fala Portuguese?*'' Luisa's voice in her own language was even more aggressive.

Jesus-Maria shook his head. He answered with chauvinistic indifference. *"Nada!"*

"But English you do speak?"

His smile was just short of sarcastic. "Reasonably well, yes."

She smoked nervously, the fumes curling through her fingers.

"Do you understand why you're here?"

I dabbed at my cheek. The oozing had stopped as well as the swelling. The formality was confusing. All this bit about him understanding why he was there. He'd been abducted and a submachine gun was stopping him from walking through the door to freedom. That was all he had to understand.

Jesus-Maria considered the palm of his hand for a second. "Reinforcements for Revolution?" he said, looking up.

Luisa's sallow cheeks colored. "You are the prisoner of The Trotsky Remembrance Movement."

The Minister's shrug was elegant, his gray green eyes mocking.

"We have a saying in Catalonia. 'You can shampoo a goat but he still smells the same.' "

She leaned hard on both elbows. "You are being held as hostage for our brothers and sisters in Valencia."

"Your friends have already told me this," he said in a level voice. "I am not impressed."

I felt in my pocket mechanically. There were two cigarettes left in the package. Giselle was stroking her throat with her fingertips, her mouth half-open. The bearded youth at the door hadn't taken his eyes off her. Christian held his hand up in the manner of Friends, Romans and Countrymen!

"May I say something?"

"You mean we have an *option?*" Abbott inquired sweetly.

Christian shot him a look of pure hatred, then turned it into a smile for Luisa.

"It's just that I'd better be thinking of moving on. I don't want to arrive at Lisbon airport like I did last time. All those flight-control numbers doing ho-hum and polishing their nails at me. Who do I see, the same man, Inspector Viola?"

Abbott batted his eyelashes. "Pocahontas doesn't want to be late for the ball. A count, no less. Biarritz will never be the same."

Christian gave a sort of whoop. "You're a shriek, Jerry, you really are!"

"Which reminds me," said Abbott. "The rest of us are supposed to have transport."

An almost transparent lizard streaked up the wall and disappeared in the reed ceiling. Luisa blew her nose on a tissue. Watering eyes gave her an appearance of sadness.

"You met a man called Seeger in Madrid?"

Abbott nodded. "You know I met him. He was my contact."

She lit one cigarette from the other and ground the spent stub into a saucer that served as ashtray.

"You made advances to him. Homosexual advances," she added primly.

He glanced across the table at Giselle but she gave him no help. He grinned nervously, like a man who heard a joke in bad taste.

"Too much. You want to check on those smackheads you've got running around up there. The advances came from him."

She exchanged brief looks with the man at the door. He popped his gum loudly and yawned.

"You lack discipline," Luisa said censoriously, a teacher addressing a rowdy classroom. "You were supposed to arrive here long before the alarm went out. Your stupidity has put lives in danger."

Giselle opened her mouth for the first time, looking directly at me. "Inspector Raven gave us no choice."

"Inspector?" Ash fell unheeded on Luisa's blouse.

"Ex-Inspector," I said, wearily, using my good eye. I'd

been saying the same thing at regular intervals over the last two days.

Luisa used another tissue, this time to clean the lenses of her spectacles.

"The plan has been changed. Beja Airfield started looking for you twenty minutes ago. Open the bag."

Abbott unzipped the blue canvas and pulled out what looked like icing sugar in a plastic sack. He slid it along the table.

"One kilo of pure scag. Courtesy of your friends in Laboratorio Hispano-Suiza."

The floorboards exuded a faint sweet smell. Carob beans had been stored in the house. Luisa put the sack in a drawer at the end of the table. That meant a kilo of uncut heroin in the hands of these lunatics. I knew enough to be sure of one thing: there was no place for apostasy in the Portuguese Communist religion. The gaunt-faced exile who now ruled had learned his gospel in Moscow. Dissidents like these, Trotskyites, would be given short shrift. Lack of a war chest had driven them to desperate ends. It all added up. A sympathizer in some Madrid drug factory, an outlet in Paris or London.

Luisa glanced from the closed drawer to me, her eyes magnified behind the powerful lenses. "A policeman," she said thoughtfully. I heard the bearded man's gum pop. She pushed her chair back and rose. The room closed in as she walked toward me.

The Minister's voice was suddenly loud. "*No!*"

It was too late. The revolver was out of her blouse and against Abbott's head. The bullet took him behind the right ear, smashing through bone into his brain. He died with his blue-shadowed eyes wide open, his face assuming an expression of great astonishment. He fell forward, his chin hitting the edge of the table. Blood saturated the back of his blond head. Then he tilted sideways, twin streams of dark red trickling from his nostrils.

Someone screamed. It was Christian. He backed off,

pushing out with both hands as Luisa moved around the table. The bearded man grabbed him from behind and held him firmly. She rammed the revolver barrel into his fall of black hair and fired. Christian rose on his toes like a ballet dancer. The man holding him stepped aside smartly. Christian collapsed, his fingers trailing down the surface of the door as if trying to retain some tactile memory of life.

My ears rang with the noise of the explosion. Burnt cordite couldn't disguise the smell of blood in my brain. I fixed my gaze on the Portuguese woman, refusing the bullet that had to be mine. She waved the revolver at me, reviving the image of a teacher in a classroom. It was the faintly regretful voice of someone obliged to punish against her will.

"These men were condemned somewhere else. I'm only the executioner."

She opened a fresh package of cigarettes, her fingers completely steady. "*Pronto,*" she said to her partner. "*Va la, filio!*"

He handed her the submachine gun and opened the door, flooding the room with the freshness of daybreak. The colors of the helicopter were vivid in the pale light. The world outside was strangely still and innocent. Dust rose as the bearded youth dragged Christian's body across the yard. The barn he took it to was no more than fifty yards away. I could see inside from where I was sitting. The man lifted the dead weight. The body hung for a second on top of the low concrete wall. A final heave sent it toppling into the pigpen. The early morning peace was shattered by an excited squealing. The bearded man trotted back like a dog retrieving a ball.

He shoved my legs to one side and bent over Abbott's corpse. Veins bulged in his neck as he heaved. He hauled the body out by the shoulders and the dust rose again in the yard. The pigs were savage now, their squabbling loud and obscene. Then mercifully the door was closed. The man took off his headband and wiped the sweat with the back of his forearm. He collected the machine gun and drank some wine from a bottle on a shelf. He was breathing heavily, his expressionless eyes on Giselle.

The Portuguese woman opened a chink in the shutters, letting light into the room. Jesus-Maria was sitting stiffly, his arms folded across his chest. Wolfie seemed to have shrunk, gray-faced under the tan. I stared at the flies buzzing around the blood on the table. And now we were four.

Giselle's giggle started deep down in her stomach, growing shriller as it gained momentum. She threw her head back suddenly and began to laugh uncontrollably. The Portuguese woman caught her on the wing with a slapping blow that jolted her into silence. Luisa's tone was conversational.

"Alvaro Saramento. Does the name mean anything to you?"

Her eyes traveled along our faces. Nobody answered. A cheap alarm clock over the fireplace showed ten minutes to five.

"He was my brother," she said. "And this was his farm. Three years ago he was murdered in cold blood, walking in peaceful procession. Shot down by the *Guarda Nacional Republicana*."

My head and body ached and the sweat dripping down my ribs was icy. I did my best not to look at her but the fascination was too strong. There were tears in her eyes. Her companion yawned.

"I want you to understand your position," she said to Jesus-Maria. "You, too, are condemned to death. The only thing that can save you is the release of the Valencia Seven."

He was tired but unafraid. "I am a cabinet minister of a friendly nation. The forces of law and order are searching for me at this very moment."

She smiled with the edges of her mouth. "The nearest forces of law and order are fifteen miles away. You are in Saramento country, my friend. Mesquita country. These people are my flesh and blood. My brother was greatly loved. Listen!" She held up a hand.

I could just see through the partly open shutters. The helicopter was jolting toward the big barn, towed by two oxen and a mule. A bent old man in a battered straw hat trudged behind, urging them on.

A certain arrogance crept in Luisa's manner. "We use your methods, Minister. But the movement has no place for degenerates. Nor are we assassins. We offer life for life."

Giselle raised her head, the hair swinging away from her face. Her hands were shaking violently.

"Did you say *degenerates!* I've spent nearly four years of my life listening to the grand aspirations of people like you, whoring for your God damn ideals with every mother's son ready to burn me or rip me off. Whatever I may be, my Portuguese friend, you're not fit to kiss my arse."

Wolfie made a halfhearted move as if to restrain her. She widened her mouth in a rictus smile.

"And that goes for you," she said to Wolfie. "It goes for all of you." Her gaze lingered on me. The contempt in it burned like acid.

It was light outside now beyond the half-open shutters. I could see a small hawk handing over the yellow sea of corn. The helicopter had been hauled into the barn. The old man and his team were out of sight along the dusty, cactus-lined lane. Pastoral scene in Iberia. It was almost unbelievable to think that two men had been killed in this room, cold-bloodedly, and fed to starving pigs: ridiculous to think that the lives of four other people were in the hands of this myopic fuzzy-haired monster in a black satin bra and *tricoteuse* cap. A swarm of blue flies had appeared from somewhere and were crawling around the edges of the dark pools of blood.

I lit my last cigarette, trying to keep my fingers steady. Luisa pointed a dirty hand at Giselle. "You talk too much. Keep your mouth shut!" The nasal whine of the last few words was perfectly done. Her English had been learned in the East End of London.

It seemed no good thinking backward or forward. The only thing to do was to concentrate on survival here and now. Wolfie was slumped with his head between his hands, a picture of a beaten man who has nowhere to go. I knew him better. His will to survive was as strong as mine. A nimble brain would be leaping behind the mask of defeat.

The bearded man moved away from the door, kicking the spent bullets across the floor. There was a tap and sink behind a flowered plastic curtain in a corner of the room together with a small stove and bottled gas. He started heating a pan of water. On the wall was a broken fragment of mirror. He studied himself in it, snipping a few hairs from his beard with a pair of nail scissors. His eyes, even in the mirror, were never off Giselle.

Luisa touched a button on the short-wave radio set. Lights showed on the fascia. She unfolded a sheet of typescript and drew her tongue through her lips.

"Do you know the call sign, MSG stroke one, Excellency?"

The coffee the bearded youth had brewed was served in thick mugs. It was strong, hot and sweet. The Minister wiped his lips with a linen handkerchieff. Stubble showed the extent of his beard and mustache.

"I know it, yes. This is the headquarters of the *Dirección General de Seguridad*, in Madrid."

She slid a packet of her tiny ciagrettes along the table. Jesus-Maria glanced at them perfunctorily and passed them on to me. She pulled the ratty looking wool cap farther down over her ears. Her eyes were quick and bright.

"There is a direct line from headquarters to the home of General Arias?"

The Minister's hands widened. "I do not know. It is probable but I cannot be certain."

"There is," she told him with assurance. She sipped her coffee, holding the mug with both hands, steam clouding her spectacles.

She wiped them and held up the typewritten sheet. "This is in Spanish. I don't speak your language but I understand it. First of all, I'm going to read you an English translation.

'This is the Trotsky Remembrance Movement speaking from Portugal. We are holding Don Jesus-Maria Alatren,

Minister for Information and Tourism, as hostage for the lives of the Valencia Seven. Alatren has been sentenced to death as a representative of Fascist Imperialism. The following terms are set for his return to Spanish territory alive and unharmed.

1) The immediate release of the Valencia Seven from the Vale de Pena Prison.
2) They will be provided with suitable civilian clothing and brought by air to Badajoz. They will be lodged on the same floor in adjoining rooms in the Golf Hotel, Badajoz.
3) General Arias will accompany them to Badajoz in person, unarmed and alone.
4) General Arias will be in communication with his headquarters at all times.
5) A further message will be sent at twenty hours Greenwich mean time giving instructions for the exchange of hostages.
6) Any violation of these terms will result in the immediate execution of Señor Jesus-Maria Alatren.

The Central Command of the Trotsky Remembrance Movement.' ''

Smoke rose between her yellowed fingers. The bearded man's mouth was half-open but he was wide-awake, keenly watching the movements of her face.

"What you are going to do now, Minister, is read the message in Spanish." She gave him a second sheet of paper.

He read it through and shrugged. "You're forgetting something. The Valencia prisoners may not *want* to be freed."

She smiled, showing a mouthful of surprisingly good teeth.

"Don't *you* want to be freed?"

She fiddled with a succession of dials, blowing smoke into the microphone as she tested it. The speaker crackled with static. She used the fine-tuner, intoning:

"M-S-G-*uno!* M-S-G-*uno!*"

A voice acknowledged the call, identifying the receiving station and standing-by. She shoved the microphone into the Minister's hands. The shadow on his cheeks was darker and his eyes were very tired. We watched in silence as a tiny red light blinked impatiently on the front of the radio. The bearded boy was standing directly opposite me, the submachine gun at the ready. I'd be the first in line when he started firing.

It seemed a lifetime before the Spaniard made his decision. He came to his feet, reading from the typewritten sheet in an easy dignified manner. He showed no emotion till the message was complete. Then he put the paper down and, still holding the microphone, said in a loud voice, "*Arriba España!*" He sat down.

"Good," said Luisa. "Empty your pockets!" She searched Giselle with nimble fingers and held the gun on us while the bearded man did the same. Luisa switched off the set, took the sack of heroin from the drawer and wrapped it in brown paper. "You have until one o'clock to rest. There will be no food until our next stop. If any one of you wants to use the lavatory, say so now. You won't have the chance later."

Giselle went first. The Portuguese woman accompanied each one of us, leaning against the wall with her pistol in hand, completely unembarrassed. The two doors led to adjoining rooms. The bushy bearded Rui ushered the Minister into one. There was a glimpse of a mattress on bare boards, of steel bars set behind the windowpanes. The man slammed the door and put the key in his pocket. The three of us were locked in the other room. The bare floor smelled of mice and carob beans. The mattresses were filled with straw, the steel bars securely cemented into thick stone walls. Outside was a weed-grown yard with an ancient midden.

Somebody hammered on the door. It was Luisa. "Don't waste your time talking to Rui. He's not only dumb, he's deaf."

Seconds later I heard the sound of a car in the lane. Then

someone coughed. This was Rui.

The sunshine was bright against the window, searching the corners of the high-ceilinged room. I half-closed the shutters, talking to myself as much as to the others. "Well, that's that."

I hadn't expected comment nor did I get any. Wolfie and Giselle were sitting on the edge of one of the mattresses, he with his arm around her. I know that love and lightning are supposed to strike anywhere but this seemed to be too much. What I was seeing embarrassed me. I started to explore the room. There was no furniture, no attempt at decoration, nothing but bare boards and walls and the two mattresses. The walls were a couple of feet thick and there wasn't even a nail in sight. The door was made of heavy planking and the lock was solid enough to secure a dungeon. On the other side of it was a killer with God alone knows what crazy thoughts stored up in his lonely head.

I knocked on the partition wall. *Did-diddy-did-did*. It was a few seconds before the man in the next room caught on, then he rapped the response. *Did-did!* Alive and well in the Alentejo. The reflection did nothing for my composure.

"Reinforcements for Revolution," I said. I couldn't help the note of sarcasm. "Congratulations!"

I could see Giselle clearly without the sunlight, the free-swinging breasts, sulky mouth and look of pure hostility. This baffled me. Alfter all, our troubles were due to her, not me. In spite of her sophisticated production she was out of her league with these hard-nosed professional revolutionaries. She was also as expendable as her colleagues had been. She measured her words and fired them at me like stones from a slingshot.

"Fuck you, Raven!"

I grinned. "Everything about you is completely charming. I wish I had the chance of learning more."

Straw rustled as Wolfie shifted his weight. "Why don't you get off her back?" he asked in a tight voice.

He had no right to my sympathy but I felt sorry for the poor bastard. She was going to destroy him. It wasn't as if he didn't know. He was hooked and there was nothing he could do about it. My feelings about her were equally ambivalent. If we had been the last two people on earth I'd have watched over her carefully, protected her from danger, the better to finally clobber her myself. I loathed this woman as someone evil and I didn't trust God or the Fate Sisters to deal with her.

Looking at her now, sitting on the bed, leaning against Wolfie's shoulder, her dark eyes challenging me, I knew that one of us *had* to go. I was determined that it wasn't going to be me.

"Why don't you hold his hand?" I suggested.

She reached out, smiling, and brought his fingers close to her mouth and nibbled them.

"Do yourself a favor and concentrate," I said to him. "If we don't think ourselves out of this one we're as good as dead."

His white suit was creased and stained, he'd lost his tie somewhere and he looked ten years older than he was. But he still hung on to her tightly, this veteran of a thousand free-for-alls with hustlers on the make and take, this connoisseur of call girls and gangsters' molls. He was actually emulating Sir Galahad, yet both of us knew that when the moment was right she would dump him. She was a natural user of men and there was no possibility of this pair going off into the sunset holding hands.

"You think they'll waste us?" he asked.

I leaned my shoulders against the wall. The swelling on my cheekbone was reduced and I could see with both eyes. "I'd say that's as certain as anything could be."

He blew hard and held out his hand for my lighter. They had left us our tobacco. "Then why haven't they already done it? What are they waiting for?"

"The right time and place," I answered. "The only person with any real chance is the guy next door. He's *not* expendable. Franco can't afford to let him go. You'll see, they'll turn those jokers loose in Valencia."

She shivered violently, whether it was real or an affectation I couldn't decide. The lady was full of surprises. I sat on the other mattress.

"You don't get on and off the air without being noticed in this day and age. Big Brother has a machine to record every word that's said. But they can't trace the source of a recorded message. It's got to be live so they can get a location fix. The authorities will be waiting for that second call tonight. This woman knows that too. That's why we're being moved."

"You think so?" Wolfie extinguished his cheroot and frugally secreted the butt.

"I *know*," I said. The tiny cigarettes were good for no more than three or four drags. "You heard what she said. This is her country. I believe her. We're about forty miles from where they're going to bring her friends. There's no river up there, just scrub and rock. A blind man and his grandmother could cross the frontier."

"How come you're suddenly an expert on Badajoz?" he asked skeptically.

"Well, I'll tell you," I said. "I'm an expert on a a hell of a lot of things that you know nothing about, Wolfie. Okay?"

He eyed me narrowly, still nursing his suspicion.

"I want to live," Giselle said quietly.

"She wants to live!" I repeated. "Fantastic! You think you have a monopoly on the thought? I don't know what sort of game you two think I'm playing but I meant every single word I said. Unless we can deal with this bastard, we're dead!"

I dropped on my knees in front of the door and peered underneath. There was a half-inch clearance at the bottom. I could see into the room beyond. The front door was wide. There was no sign of the deaf mute. Dust floated in the sunlight. I tiptoed across to the shutters and looked through the crack. The bearded man was standing on top of a muckheap, ankle-deep in nettles, trying to see into the room. I sat down on the mattress again, lit another Portuguese cigarette and looked Wolfie straight in the eye.

"That subhuman out there fancies your girl. It's our only chance of getting out of here."

The struggle taking place in his mind showed in his face. "And if we do make it?"

I didn't take his point. "Then we're alive. How do you mean if we do make it?"

"I want to know what happens to Giselle and me," he said in a level voice. "We were on our way to Brazil."

He made it sound as if he'd been put to great personal inconvenience.

"Bully for you," I said. "She'll fuck up there just as well as any other place. If we manage to take the Minister with us I'll guarantee that neither of you will be prosecuted."

They looked at one another. "Do you trust him?" she asked.

He moved his shoulders uncertainly. "I always have." It wasn't strictly true but I knew what he meant. The difference was that I no longer trusted him.

She turned her head toward me. "Tell me what you want me to do."

I moved to the other mattress. The man outside was supposed to be deaf and dumb but I kept my voice down. A woman like Giselle didn't need my advice. She'd been chopping men off at the ankles all her life. But she listened attentively to my instructions, widening and narrowing her eyes, nestling into Wolfie's protective arm. I'd no way of being sure what was in her mind at that moment but Wolfie and I were predictable. I'd already judged her. All that was left was to fix the punishment. To protect her against it, Wolfie would kill me if necessary. Nevertheless we went through the motions of being allies if not comrades.

She slipped out of Wolfie's embrace, bend down and kissed him on the mouth. Her eyes were half-closed as she straightened up but I caught the challenge in them. No matter what else she was thinking, this much was clear. Wolfie was her property. She opened the shutters. Wolfie and I were prone on the mattresses, faking sleep. She tapped on the windowpane.

"Louder," I said. "He's deaf."

Her fingernails rattled on the glass. I sneaked a look from my position on the floor. She was standing in front of the window, pantomiming two men sleeping. I could hear the Minister moving about in the next room. She closed the shutters again, dimming the room.

"He's coming."

She ran across the room and stationed herself, leaning against the wall facing the door. I was lying on the mattress near to her, Wolfie next to me, curled up in a foetal position. The moments stretched. I heard the creak of floorboards, than a shadow fell across the streak of light at the bottom of the door. The key was carefully inserted in the lock, the tip just showing inside the room. The bearded man had the sense of feel of the blind. The key slowly revolved, lifting the heavy tumblers and withdrawing the tongue from the cup. He started to push the door open. I could see his thick-soled shoes with bulbous toecaps and brass eyelets. Then the handle was turned with exquisite care, leaving the door ajar.

Giselle stayed where she was, smiling, her dark hair falling across her face. The crack widened. Looking up, I saw an arm come through, the blunt suntanned fingers reaching for the woman against the wall. I hurled myself against the door, my full weight behind it. The door caught his arm against the jamb like a nutcracker. I heard the bone snap, the yelp of pain. I pulled the door back. Wolfie was up on his feet beside me. The bearded man was on his knees facing us, his right arm bangling uselessly, snarling like an animal. He puckered up his lips as Giselle came through the doorway and spat like a cobra. She kept going, wiping the spittle from her face and kicking the submachine gun away as he grabbed for it with his good hand. Wolfie brought the chair down hard. It flew apart, framing the kneeling man with the remnants of the seat. He fell sideways, shutting his eyes with a sort of ferocious resignation. I found some cord in a cupboard and we trussed him up, face down, between the two mattresses. I closed the shutters and turned the key on him. With luck someone would find him. The Devil was supposed to take care of his own. If not, tough titty.

Back in the main room, we looked at one another in a silence broken only by the buzzing of the flies over the pools of congealed blood. Sunshine streamed through the open doorway. I picked up the submachine gun, trying to look as if I knew how to handle it. There were Russian or Czech markings on the stock and barrel.

Jesus-Maria shouted from behind his door. "*Qué pasa?*"

The key was missing, probably somewhere in the mattress sandwich. I signaled to Wolfie and shouted back.

"Stand away from the door!"

We used our shoulders as battering rams, hitting the door at the same time. It collapsed, leaving the lock dangling by the tongue. Jesus-Maria stepped out over the splintered wood. The stubble of beard was dark against his face but he was smiling. His eyes searched the room. I nodded at the other door.

"In there. He won't bother us."

"*My bien, hombre,*" he said with satisfaction.

I gave him the submachine gun. He'd know as much about it as I did and the weapon was safer with him. The short-wave radio set had vanished and so had the heroin. It was almost eleven by the alarm clock over the fireplace. I found the two handguns in the drawer at the end of the table. I gave Wolfie his and kept Abbott's Walther. Giselle watched with eyes smudged by fatigue. Each of us knew what the other was thinking.

10

"Now what?" said Jesus-Maria.

"The first thing is to get the hell out of here," I answered.

He nodded. The other two just stared. "There's no phone and there's no food," I added. "I'm going to see if there's any transportation."

I walked out into the blinding sunshine and followed the tracks where the helicopter had been dragged out of sight of aerial reconnaissance. The pigs in the adjoining barn set up a racket. I shut my mind to them and looked for a hammer. There was a blunted pickax hanging on a nail. I took it and chambered up on top of the helicopter cabin. By the time I'd finished with the two gas turbine engines they wouldn't have lifted a feather from the ground. The windmill up on the hill turned its blades lazily, shimmering in the heat haze. The hawk hung high above the sea of yellow corn, the only living thing in sight apart from the pigs. I trotted back across the yard.

"There's no car," I told them. "Not even a bicycle."

"She'll be back," Jesus-Maria said with assurances. "Won't she, Señorita?" The question was for Giselle, a subtle reminder of whose side she was meant to be on. She

163

raised her chin slowly, looking at him. I don't know why but he was the only one she hadn't stroked with her eyes. Maybe she knew that he was unreachable.

"She'll be back," she answered quietly.

Wolfie was going to say something but thought better of it. He didn't have to tell me. He wanted to make a deal but he wasn't sure how. I spread my hands.

"We won't last long on the roads. Our only chance is to stick to the corn fields. Do you agree or not?"

"Agreed," said Jesus-Maria. Wolfie stuck his thumb up. Giselle tied her hair in her scarf.

We left the front door open and walked round to the back of the farmhouse. The stream curled away behind the hill before bisecting the corn fields. I pointed down the lush bank over-grown with wild freesia.

"If we wade upstream, we won't break the corn at the edges. There'll be no sign of us going in."

We took off our socks and shoes and rolled up our pants. The water was very cold and the color of weak tea. It rose to my knees, tiny transparent fish darting away as I moved against the current, mud sucking at the soles of my feet. Giselle was close to the bank, the Minister and Wolfie behind me. Jesus-Maria was wading like some gung-ho hero coming ashore, the machine gun held high above his head. I remember thinking that if he tripped he'd take our heads off.

We waded upstream for a couple of hundred yards till the hill lay between us and the farmhouse. The thought somehow made me feel better. Trees were growing out of the bank at the bend. I clambered up over exposed roots to the edge of the corn field. The grain grew straight and dense, almost up to my shoulders. The hawk had been circling high overhead as if watching our progress. I watched it wheel and plane away till it was finally lost in the haze.

The others were still standing knee-deep in the water, in the shade of the leafy branches. Wolfie tucked his gun in his waistband, using both hands to splash his face and then drink. Brilliantly colored dragonflies darted voraciously over the flowing surface, trapping insects in flight.

"We'd better go in here," I suggested, pushing my thumb at the yellow forest of corn in front of me. I wasn't sure who was meant to be leader, Jesus-Maria or me.

He was standing splay-legged in the stream. His silk suit was soaked and dappled sunshine fell across his face.

"Would it not be better to stay?" he said. "The water leaves no trace."

I pointed vaguely east. "Where there's water there's life. There'll be other farms, animals, dogs. Let's keep under cover as much as we can."

I gave him my hand and he climbed up the bank. Wolfie did the same for Giselle. We were an odd-looking bunch, tired and unshaved, water dripping from our clothes. Jesus-Maria plucked a head of corn, rolled it in his palms and blew away the husks. His teeth closed on the kernels. As they did, he winked. And I suddenly realized that he was enjoying himself. We put on our socks and shoes.

I pointed again, this time toward the distant telephone poles. "I'm going first. I want you to keep in single file, ready to duck when I go like this." I chopped down with my arm.

Once we were in, I pushed back past them and pulled the flattened corn upright. It was all I could do. I hoped it would be enough unless they used dogs to track us down. It was hard work in front, parting the sturdy stalks, the sharp-bladed grass tearing at my hands and clothing. Dust tickled my throat and nostrils. I sneezed violently. All I needed now was a bout of hay fever. My antihistamine pills were back at the bungalow. After a hundred yards or so I hit a dry stone wall about four feet high dividing one field from another. I followed it along to a gap and set a diagonal course across the neighboring stand of corn. Anyone looking would have seen no more than our heads and shoulders. But there was no one *to* see, no more than a couple of hares, disturbed at their feeding and jack-knifing back along our trail. Butterflies rose and floated as we pushed on under the relentless sun. We were all carrying our jackets. My shirt and trousers had long since dried and were wet again, this time with sweat. It prickled on my legs, reviving the smart of the old jellyfish stings. Jesus-Maria was close behind me, his tread firm and easy and I knew that he was going to outlast us all.

We must have covered three miles, clambering over stone walls, negotiating a gate hidden in the tangle of corn, surprising a dog-fox sleeping in an unused lane. The telephone poles were much nearer now, no more than five hundred yards away. I signaled everyone to duck low as we approached the edge of the field. I crawled forward on my hands and knees and parted the stalks. We were within spitting distance of a narrow cobbled road that ran like a plumb line through the fields to an incline crowned with whitewashed buildings. I could see a church like a fortress, more Spanish than Portuguese, a ruined tower with battlements. Flowers grew on both sides of the road. A concrete marker among them named the town: LUDO 1 km.

The telephone poles marched with the flowers and the cobblestones were gray, polished and timeless. I rolled over to face the others.

"It's some kind of small town. I can see a bridge over a river. I'm going to head for somewhere near there."

Bits of grass were caught in Giselle's hair where the scarf had failed to protect it. Her trousers were torn above the knee. Wolfie covered the bare flesh possessively.

"We need food, whatever else. Food and drink."

I nodded in the direction of the river. "Forget about food for the moment. There's water over there. The question is, are we going to risk a telephone?"

Jesus-Maria was lying flat on his stomach, the machine-gun under his chest. He switched the blade of grass from one side of his mouth to the other. "Tell me what *you* think!"

I blew the dust out of my nostrils. "The first thing is to get away from this road."

We crawled back on our tracks. They sprawled. I sat with

my hands locked around my knees.

"Number one. We'd better make up our minds that we *have* no friends. Every farmer, every uniform, the old biddies with shawls over their heads, they'll all be looking for us. In my book the authorities are only marginally better than Luisa's team. You're Spanish, a member of what the Portuguese have publicly called a repressive régime. Once they find you they're going to throw you in some high-class jail and make a scandal about your presence in the country. And they'll find a thousand and one reasons for putting us there with you. On the other hand, we're no more than forty miles from the frontier. That's less than an hour if we can find a car."

He rubbed his stubbled chin thoughtfully. "We need documents to hire a car, and Portuguese money."

I moved a forefinger from side to side. "We don't hire. We *steal!* Just as soon as it's dark. In the meantime we rest. If there's chance of good, okay. If not, we'll survive."

Wolfie lifted his head from Giselle's lap. "If you want my opinion . . ."

"We don't," I said. He put his head back. I looked from him to Jesus-Maria. "The alternative is that we split with everyone going his own way. It's up to you."

"We're staying," Wolfie put in quickly. Giselle nodded, her eyes on Jesus-Maria.

The Minister smiled, showing his fine teeth. "It is agreed then. You are our leader."

I had his trust, there was no question of it. I was glad that this was the way it would be. I held out my hand to Wolfie. "I'll take the gun."

A truck rattled along the road, the tires hissing over the cobbles. "What's the matter," he said. "Don't you trust me?"

It was the old easy grin but his eyes held a hint of despair as if he realized that every judgment he made was the wrong one.

"Not any more," I said. Giselle's fingers were hidden

behind his back but I guessed that they were encouraging him.

He shrugged and placed the gun in my outstretched palm. "Win a few, lose a few."

Jesus-Maria turned his wrist, consulting his watch. He had too much style to be a back-seat driver but I could imagine what he was thinking. It was a long time till nightfall and during the intervening hours decisions would be taken on his behalf, his career and worth would be weighed against the Valencia Seven. There'd be no doubt of the outcome but his dignity would have been placed in jeopardy. And to a Spaniard of his class, dignity mattered above all else.

"Let's move," I said quietly. "And keep your heads low."

The stand of wheat stretched down toward the river, thinning as the grass grew stonier. They came to a halt while I crawled to the edge of the field. The sluggish river lay below, bright in the sunshine, its banks overhung with cane. A couple of hundred yards away, a Roman bridge led the cobbled road into the small town. A girl was washing clothes on a flat rock close to the bridge. Sheets were drying on the bushes behind her. The ruined tower rose on the opposite bank, the massive church behind it. I crawled back and made my report.

Jesus-Maria picked a wriggling inch of something from his monogrammed shirt and squashed it with a stone. My mind was on scorpions but I preferred not to see. He wiped his fingers fastidiously with his handkerchief, gazing across the river. Half a mile away, a mechanical harvester was scything through the wheat crop.

He put his handkerchief back in his jacket pocket. "We can't go on. There is no more cover."

"We're staying here," I assured him. "I'm going to have a closer look at things and get some water."

I took the submachine gun from his knees. He made no attempt to stop me but Wolfie cocked his eyebrows.

"Now what?"

There was an edge of fear to his voice that embarrassed

me. We'd come that far apart but I was sure that I was doing the right thing.

"I told you," I answered. "I'm going to take a closer look. I want to see how the land lies."

Jesus-Maria checked his clip in the hand gun I'd given him. This time there was no doubt. He knew exactly what he was about. The way he did it, the look he gave me, were affirmations of his solidarity.

I crept to the top of the bank. The barelegged girl below was spreading wet wash over the bushes with her back to me. I made it down to the screen of reeds in seconds, hung my socks and shoes around my neck and crouched ankle-deep in the soft warm mud. A bell tolled in the church clock, the cracked metallic sound echoing under the bridge. I sank the submachine gun in the mud and pushed out into deeper water. The river was low in a bed of stones ground smooth by time. I forded it, going up to my knees in places, hidden from the girl by a bend in the bank. The reeds were thicker on the other side. I waded out past rusted buckets, chewed tires, a dead cat with a bell around its neck and a gas-distended belly. I sat on the slope and put my shoes back on. A hobbled mule was cropping the grass a few yards away, flicking the fields with its tail. The ruined tower was immediately above me. The roof and rafters had collapsed but the stone circular staircase was intact. The well was obviously used as a rubbish dump. I climbed a hundred feet to what was left of the battlements. The small town nestled about a square in front of the church. I could see a bandstand, a couple of cafés, the Portuguese flag hanging outside what looked like a police barracks. A bus was unloading in front of a garage. The square trapped the noonday heat, channeling it into the warren of narrow streets.

Everything seemed to move at half-speed, the figures crossing the steps in front of the church, a running dog, a truck top-heavy with timber. There were a dozen cars or more parked near the bandstand. Two men dressed in the gray uniform of the *Guàrda Nacional* left the police building *dressing* in sun helmets and carrying carbines. I watched them to a Land-Rover that was driven fast out of town on the east-bound road. The church clock banged again, marking the passage of another quarter-hour. I walked along the battlements, keeping as low as possible. There was a clear view of the south bank of the river and the wheat field above it. I tried to locate our hiding place and failed. As long as we kept our heads we were safe there. I could see cottages up toward the bridge, whitewashed shacks splashed with color where flowers grew. All of them looked deserted, the occupants probably at work in the fields. But stealing food was clearly out of the question.

I found four empty wine bottles in the well of the tower and made my way down to the river. My bare feet felt good in the mud. The washing was still spread over the bushes but the girl had gone. I rinsed the bottles and filled them from the middle of the stream. A couple of minutes later I was back where the others were hiding in the wheat field. There was a bottle of water apiece. Giselle sipped from hers before cupping her hands and using them to wash her face. Jesus-Maria gargled and spat out the water as a fighter does between rounds. Wolfie just finished the bottle.

We were sprawling on the ground with the wheat stalks flattened around us. An airplane droned overhead, flying too low and slow to be anything but a commercial flight on its way from Lisbon to Faro.

Jesus-Maria shook his jacket into a sort of pillow and stared after the plane. His collar was undone, revealing a lapis lazuli cross on a gold chain. The hair on his chest grew thick like that on his forearms. He half-closed his eyes.

"You are gambling, Señorita."

Wolfie was lying flat with Giselle's head resting against his thigh. I was the only one sitting up and could see the expression on their faces. Wolfie's jaw muscles tightened. Giselle raised an arm in a gesture of acceptance.

"We're all gambling. You included."

The sounds of the town drifted over the river: a truck rumbling across the bridge, children's voices, a dog barking.

Jesus-Maria stretched and yawned.

"Do you have family, Señorita? A father, perhaps, a mother?"

She answered from the shelter of Wolfie's elbow. "Both. And I played with dolls and made my first communion."

Jesus-Maria thought about that for a while and smiled, "I am very glad I do not have a daughter like you."

Wolfie's grip tightened on her. "You gave us your word, Raven, remember. I want to hear it from him."

I took a swig from my bottle. The water tasted alkaline. "If it hadn't been for them we wouldn't have made it, Minister." I thought of him as Jesus-Maria but in English it sounded ridiculous. "They've no more chance here now than we have."

Both statements were true but my concern for Wolfie was a lot less than it appeared to be.

He opened his eyes wide at me. I nodded. "I gave them my word that they won't be prosecuted in Spain. It's part of the deal. I'm sorry but it has to be that way."

He gave me a long look before stretching again and smiling. "*Bueno!* I give them twenty-four hours to leave my country."

He had the sort of panache that I admired. Here he was lying in a wheat field in the heart of militant Communism, hunted by unbalanced fanatics, yet he was able to dispense favors with the condescension of a conquering hero.

"Fair enough?" I asked Wolfie.

"Fair enough," he answered.

We pooled our smoking material. Four cheroots, a couple of bent cigarettes smelling of Estée Lauder out of Giselle's bag, the remains of the Portuguese packet. I made the division and settled down on my jacket. Jesus-Maria had concealed his gun. I stuffed mine down the front of my trousers. I'd no idea what stunt Wolfie and Giselle might have in mind. As far as I could see they needed us. But instinct prompted mistrust.

I dozed, thinking of Cathy again. It seemed that the last

few days had released memories that had been submerged for years. Above all there was a feeling of guilt, that I'd failed the one person in my life who had really mattered. I waked suddenly, coming up on an elbow to see Giselle pushing back through the wheat. Jesus-Maria's slitted eyes registered her return. Wolfie took her in his arms again. The sun had gone. Birds were setting up a racket in the twilight. It was almost nine o'clock. We had dozed, slept or rested for the best part of eight hours. None of us had eaten since early that morning but I was past hunger. I sat up and drank some water. The wind was blowing away from the river. I lit Wolfie's cheroot. He was busy combing his hair while Jesus-Maria was rubbing the circulation back into his legs. The stubble was black on his face. He grinned as if he knew what was on my mind.

"As a policeman you would arrest me on sight, no?"

"I'd arrest the lot of us," I said. "No questions asked. And you'd be favorite. I'd have the cuffs on you before I took any chances."

Wolfie's white suit was a mess, his buckskin shoes scarred and scuffed. Giselle came out the most presentable of all. She'd pushed her hair up into her scarf and used her lipstick. Jesus-Maria smiled apologetically as his stomach rumbled. I rose, aware of their expectancy. I'd never in my life fancied myself as a leader and least of all now. The fat-eared wheat stood straight and still in the fading light. The ruined tower was etched against the violet sky. Lamps burned in the shacks on the opposite bank, yellow squares strung along the river side. A strip of blinking neon located the café in front of the dark mass of the church. I'd transferred the gun to my jacket, it sagged in the right-hand pocket.

"Okay. Here's the plan. You three are going to cross that bridge at intervals of two minutes and make for that tower. You wait there till I arrive."

They were up on their feet, standing close behind me, gazing over my shoulder at the river and the lights beyond.

"Do you really think you could manage to lift one of those cars?" Wolfie sounded doubtful.

I dropped the cheroot in the dirt. I was near the end and it was making my mouth bitter.

"You'd be surprised what I can do." I pointed in the direction of the church. "See that road, the one with the street lamps? That's our way out. I want you to wait in the tower till you see me. Don't move. Is that understood?"

Jesus-Maria put his hand on my shoulder. "We will do what you say, *amigo*. Have confidence in me."

I shoved my fingers through my hair and buttoned my jacket. "If I'm not back in an hour's time, you're on your own."

"Good luck," he said and smiled. "Be careful."

I cut through the wheat to the side of road, emerging about fifty yards away from the bridge. A lamp was burning at each end of the single span. A car passed as I crossed, going in the opposite direction. I looked straight ahead, listening to the dwindling sound of its motor. The narrow streets on the far side of the bridge were still warm from the sun, the smell of cooking coming from the doorways. I could hear the blare of television. A man wearing a leather cap kicked a motorcyle to life and stuttered away toward the square. I followed. The square was larger than it had seemed from the tower. On the north side wide steps ascended to the buttressed church that was built of the rock it stood on. Heavy old houses with flowers growing on sagging varandahs leaned forward precariously. A violet neon strip rippled above a window filled with notices of football matches, bullfights and bus schedules: *Café Alentejo*.

Two yellow-sweatered youngsters were shooting bar-pool beyond the beaded curtain hinging in the entrance. Others were playing the pinball machine. A relief map was modeled on the wall behind the pumps in the gas station. The road I wanted ran due east to a place called Almobar. The frontier was only thirty miles away.

A couple of Republican Guards came out of the police station, sturdy looking in black leather leggings, their faces remote under sharply peaked caps. I turned quickly, away from the lights of the café and the gas station and walked down between the orange trees. Old men were sitting on the benches exchanging memories under faded political slogans: *Viva Spinola! A people united can never be defeated! Death to the Fascists!*

The hammer and sickle was stenciled everywhere, on the front of the church, the trunks of the trees and the tiled esplanade.

I found an empty bench near the steps. The church doors were open. A smell of stale incense drifted out from the dark interior. I sat in the shadows, thinking about stealing transport. They show you the tricks of the trade in police college, demonstrating how a burglar wields a plastic playing card to open a spring lock, the use of cuttlefish bone to take impressions of keys and the like. After eighteen years on the Force, there was little about this sort of caper I hadn't experienced. But I'd never hot-wired a car. Looking at the line of vehicles parked under the orange trees, I was a whole lot less confident than I had been in the wheat field.

It was well after nine. Anything that Interpol could or would do on my behalf no longer mattered. My future was linked to Jesus-Maria. The facts were that a Spanish Cabinet minister had been abducted at pistol-point in full view of his security forces, the conditions for his return made from a neighboring and no longer so friendly country. Every Spanish frontier post would have been alerted hours ago.

A pickup truck turned into the square, overloaded with men wearing red armbands. They were carrying weapons ranging from shotguns to pistols. The truck stopped in front of the café and someone shouted into a loudspeaker. The words bounced bak from the fronts of the overhung houses. The short speech was full of bussings, of exploded consonants and nasal vowel sounds. The speaker used a word repeatedly that I recognized. *Vigilantes*. I remember the piece I had read the week before about something that had happened in Lisbon. Men with armbands had burst into the house of a newspaper editor and pulled him out of his bed.

They'd told his terrified wife that no warrant was needed for dealing with enemies of the people and had shot him through the head three times. The speaker bawled his final address: *Viva Portugal!*

The youths crowding the doorway of the café responded but the old men sitting on the benches were silent. The truck roared off in the direction of the bridge below. I wiped my neck and forehead with my handkerchief. In spite of the time it was hot and there wasn't a whisper of a breeze. Worse still, the moon rising behind the fortresslike church flooded the wheat fields beyond with pale clear light.

Only twenty minutes had passed since I had left the others but it seemed much longer. The one thing I couldn't afford to do was get myself caught in the act of driving someone else's car away. There was no room for failure. I watched a battered Mercedes arrive, knowing instinctively that its owner would lock it. He did. A panel truck turned in after him, its head-lamps searching the bench I was sitting on. I covered my face with my hands. The headlamps went out and the motor stopped. I peeped between my fingers. A sunburned man in overalls jumped down from the cab and slammed the door behind him. He walked away toward the café. I followed, keeping to the other side of the square and watched him through the bead curtains. I waited there till I saw him with a cue in his hands, then I hurried back and opened the door of the panel truck.

The back was empty, a greasy paper bag on the seat smelled of garlic. The keys were gone. I opened the paper bag and ate the remains of the sandwich. I had no knife and there were no tools in the glove compartment. I bent down, groping under the dash till I found the two wires behind the ignition lock. I yanked them out and used my thumbnails to bare the copper. Sweat was running into my eyes and my back expected a tap at any moment. I couldn't see but I felt, joining the two tiny loops. The motor responded im-mediately. In spite of the sudden clatter, I released the hand brake gently as if the operation would bring the old men to

175

their feet shouting alarm. Not a head turned.

I drove out of the square and down toward the bridge. The ruined tower was stark behind the dark houses. Suddenly a man stepped from a doorway, his arm outstretched, pointing. Another step brought him into the road. Either I stopped or knocked him down. I braked hard and felt for the gun in my pocket. There was no alternative. He didn't know it but he was going to be a passenger. Then I heard him yell, still pointing at the front of the car.

"*Luz!*"

I fumbled for the switch, realizing that my lights were off. He blinked in the sudden blaze, nodded and stepped back onto the pavement. I drove on slowly, accelerating as I turned the lane by the side of the moonlit river. Dust rose in front and behind. A dog snarled. I could see it, chained in front of one of the cottages, stiff-legged and straining. I spun the wheel, turning in front of the tower. Three figures emerged as I threw the cab door open. Giselle and Wolfie clambered over the seat into the back. Jesus-Maria sat beside me. His teeth flashed in his dark face.

"Keep down," I said over my shoulder. The truck shot forward as I put my foot on the pedal.

It was a strange drive. The front shock absorbers had just about had it and the truck bucked on the bends like a bronco. Jesus-Maria and Wolfie had cleaned themselves up. If you ignored their beards they looked almost respectable. No one seemed to want to talk. There was practically no traffic on the road. I told Jesus-Maria about the vigilantes I'd seen. His eyes narrowed.

"Aiee! Which way did they go?"

A sign flicked by, ALMOBAR 8 km. "Over the bridge. In the direction of the farmhouse. You think they were looking for us?"

He wriggled a shoulder. "Who knows? These people are animals, mad dogs that attack without reason. They even turn on themselves."

I peeked in the rearview mirror. Giselle's eyes were fixed

on mine, watchful and telling nothing. The flat fields on each side of the highway had been harvested. Pyramids of baled straw towered in the moonlight. The tires whined as we ran onto a cobbled surface. A concrete marker on the shoulder of the road read, ESPANHA 1 km.

I pulled the truck off onto a rough lane. We jolted up into the shelter of a three-sided barn. I pulled the ignition wires apart, silencing the motor.

"Spain," I nodded.

I could feel Giselle's breath on my neck and smell her scent as she leaned forward, peering through the windshield. Almobar was no more than a huddle of blank-faced shacks petering out fifty yards from the brilliantly lit frontier post. The buildings were designed in two units. Left were the customs and passport offices, a bank and tourist bureau on the other side of the road. The latter two were closed. There were covered bays for the reception of motorized traffic. There were no vehicles in sight, no sign of movement anywhere.

"It's closed." Giselle's voice was strangely resigned.

"No," said Wolfie. "I can see two guys, over on the left, smoking."

I followed his finger. The were leaning against the wall under the arch, dressed in what looked like naval uniforms.

Jesus-Maria started what surely had to be the last smoke he had. I'd finished mine long since.

"Passport-control," he said. "But the post still might be closed."

A hundred yards of floodlit highway separated the two frontier posts. The pole barriers were down on each side. The Spanish buildings were in white concrete. The red and yellow ensign hung above a shield emblazoned with the double eagle. A thick-set cop wearing dark glasses was sitting on a chair reading a newspaper.

Jesus-Maria felt in an inside pocket and displayed an identity card in his palm. "Alatren y Martorell. In Spain we put the mother's name after the father's. But not in Portugal.

177

The name Martorell will mean nothing to them. You have some identification?''

I showed him my international driver's license. ''Only this. They took care of the rest.''

Jesus-Maria looked at them questioningly. ''You have passports?''

Wolfie nodded. Giselle raised her bag in answer.

''Dale or Degenhardt?'' I asked. I couldn't resist it. Jesus-Maria glanced from her to me. He hadn't understood and it was no time to explain.

''Forget it.'' I pointed at the empty fields in front of us. ''That's Spain, right?''

He moved his shoulders uncertainly. ''The distance I do not know but near, yes.''

The village houses were shuttered. There was nothing under the moonlight but the brilliant frontier posts and open ground. I found a piece of paper and gave him my pen.

''Now listen carefully. I want you to write something that will show who you are. I'm going to take your identity card with me.''

Doubt showed in his face. ''But why alone? If you can go, why not all of us?''

''If it's that easy we will,'' I promised. ''But not before I see what we have out there.''

He scribbled something, folded the piece of paper inside the identity card and gave it to me. The barn was half-filled with straw, the piled bales concealing the truck from anyone on the road. I let myself out of the cab, gave them a look that was meant to reassure them and worked my way around the blind side of the barn. I peeked from the corner. The two men at the Portuguese frontier post had gone inside. I started to run, bending as low as I could. I sweated and floundered, slipping on the sheared wheat stalks. Two hundred yards, three. Then I was down on my knees in the moonlight, every ache and itch in my body revived. I knelt there, taking my weight on my hands, looking at the tangle of barbed wire in front of me. It stretched left and right, as high as a horse and four feet wide. The barbs were razor-edged instead of being pointed. I pulled myself up and headed for the barn. Jesus-Maria had the cab door open, his face anxious in the half-light. I climbed in and stuck the identity card in his hand.

"There's wire," I said. "We'd need a tank to go through it, I'm sorry."

I heard Wolfie suck his breath in. There was trouble in his voice as he leaned forward. "So what are we supposed to do?"

The resentment of the last few days made my answer savage. "What do you mean, what are *we* supposed to do! You ought to know, you've been manipulating people all your bloody life. Ask the woman you're supposed to be in love with."

He stared back blankly and I could tell that he was genuinely shocked. His arm pulled Giselle closer.

"Why don't you say it?" he challenged. "It's been on your mind long enough. I'm a Jew and you don't like Jews. That's your real hang-up, isn't it?"

I shook my head. "You're nothing, Wolfie. I don't worry about you any more. You're not worth it."

Something moved in the bales of straw, a rat or a rabbit, something that rustled through the darkness and crouched there listening to us.

Giselle's voice was almost shy. "I could walk into that office, a woman alone. I could get their attention. You'd be on the Spanish side before they knew what happened."

We looked out instinctively toward the lights, at the empty road stretching back through endless fields glimmering under the moon. The no man's land between the frontier posts. There was nothing to be seen through the uncurtained windows by the arch on the Portuguese side. Nobody said anything.

She went on with quite sincerity. "I could do it, I know. Not for you, for Wolfie. Give us that chance, at least. You'd be in Spain. I'll be all right. My passport's in order. I'll give them some story."

I don't know where his courage came from but Wolfie found it. His grip tightened on her shoulder. "No way. If you go, I go."

I could see her face in the rearview mirror. The smile of resignation faded with her voice. "You don't trust me, do you?"

It was somehow better than the answer came from Jesus-Maria. He delivered it with a finality that put the issue beyond doubt.

"No, Señorita, I do not trust you."

The straw behind the truck rustled again. A dog howled in the distance. Every sound marked the passage of time in my head. I was thinking of the suntanned man in the café, putting his cue down and walking out into the night, crossing the square under the orange trees, past the old men on the benches to where he had left his truck. Jesus-Maria undid the door on his side.

"We must go," he said firmly. "If we stay here we are lost."

I felt as if I was being left behind and it wasn't a good feeling. Some of it sounded in my voice.

"I don't know if you remember but all I have is a driver's license. I don't see them taking a look at it and waving me on."

Jesus-Maria put his hand on my arm. "We are three men. They are only two. There is no other way, my friend."

I let my breath go. There are times when a man is happy to shed the weight of responsibility.

We walked out of the barn together. We stayed abreast until we reached the group of white buildings. Jesus-Maria dropped behind the other two as we passed the shuttered bank and tourist office. The pole barrier marked the floodlit span between the two frontier posts. The Spanish cop was still sitting on his chair reading the newspaper. Giselle knocked on the door of the passport office. A man's face appeared at the window, a young face with a bristle of blue black hair over snapping suspicious eyes. His voice was clear through the open window.

"*Fechado!*"

"Closed," muttered Jesus-Maria.

The official shifted to one side, angling his head to get a better view of the road behind us. He was looking for the car that had brought us, some sort of conveyance. A second official appeared, an older man wearing thick-framed spectacles. He put his head near the window and inspected us.

"*Fechado!*" he repeated.

My voice echoed under the archway. "Do you speak any English?"

A key turned and the two men stood in the open doorway. I could see a desk with two revolver holsters, the butts of the weapons showing. There was a telephone and some kind of high-powered radio set with earphones. The spectacled man took a backward step. He was gray haired with sleep-filled eyes.

"In the morning you return. Come again." There was a clock behind him on the wall and he put a finger on the dial. "Eight o'clock, you come back. Now is closed."

Giselle stepped through the doorway, her eyes smiling at the younger man. Wolfie followed. Jesus-Maria nudged me forward. The radio headphones were hanging on the back of a chair near the table.

"Tomorrow," the older man emphasized.

Giselle moved close to the younger man's side. Her voice was accusing as she pointed at Jesus-Maria.

"This one is the Spanish minister. The other two are fascists."

We seemed to feeeze for a time, then the man next to Giselle seized a revolver from its holster. I can remember Wolfie's face as he looked at Giselle for the last time. Then he turned and ran. The shot hit him in the nape of the neck. His impetus carried him on through the doorway. He collapsed outside and lay on the ground, his body jerking. Than he was still. He died as he had lived, gambling. What he'd finally lost was his self-respect. My own was tarnished but

181

still intact.

I wrestled the gun out of my pocket but Jesus-Maria was first, firing across the room. The younger official fell, grabbing at his leg, blood gushing through his fingers. His partner pushed his hands high in the air, his toes rising in sympathy. His face had gone old and gray, his spectacles smashed at his feet. I yanked the phone wires from the wall and toppled the radio set onto the floor. It broke in pieces. Jesus-Maria kicked them aside.

"Quickly!" he urged.

I caught Giselle as she snatched at the second revolver holster, getting her with a flat-handed blow that sent her reeling off balance. I was onto her quickly, avoiding her shrewdly intended kick. I grabbed her wrist and forced her arm up behind her. Then I shoved her forward in a scrambling run, dusking under the barrier and into the blaze of light illuminating the stretch of no man's land. Jesus-Maria was twenty yards in front of us, yelling in Spanish and waving frantically. There was sweat in my eyes but I could see the doors opening in the buildings on the far side of the lifting barrier, a blur of gray-clad figures. And suddenly we were in Spain. I pulled Giselle down on the bench by the wall, fighting for breath. The red and yellow flag drooped above the Hapsburg eagle. My mouth and nostrils were acrid from the explosions. Jesus-Maria was talking to a civilian in dark clothes, his shoulders expressive. They both turned and started toward us. The official's face was cold and implacable.

Giselle's voice seemed to come from another place and time. "Help me, Raven. I'll be whatever you want but help me."

There were nearing us now, flanked by a group of frontier police. Her dark eyes mirrored my stare, her lips uncertain. The lie she sought evaded her. There was nothing left but supplication.

"Help me," she whispered.

Revenge, punishment, call it what you will, the moment I

had waited for had fallen strangely flat. All I knew was that I was tired, hungry and dirty.

"On your feet," I said.

They took her into a room with bars on the windows, still swinging her hips as she went through the doorway. It was the last I saw of her. I took the cigarette from Jesus-Maria's outstretched hand and followed him into the office.

www.ingramcontent.com/pod-product-compliance
Ingram Content Group UK Ltd.
Pitfield, Milton Keynes, MK11 3LW, UK
UKHW022311280225
455674UK00004B/266